The Taste of Snow

*"I will honor Christmas in my heart,
and try to keep it all the year."*

— CHARLES DICKENS

The Taste of Snow

by Stephen V. Masse

GOOD HARBOR PRESS

THE TASTE OF SNOW
Copyright 2012 by Stephen V. Masse

This is a work of fiction. Names, characters, places and incidents are the product of the author's imagination or are used fictitiously.

Good Harbor Press
80 Walsh Street
Medford, MA 02155
www.goodharborpress.com

Cover design and illustrations by Brian Allen
www.flylanddesigns.com

The text of this book was set in ITC New Baskerville

Book design by Michel Newkirk

Printed in the United States of America

Library of Congress Control Number 2011928294
ISBN 13   978-0-9799638-1-0

Dedicated to the fond memory of
Mary Ann Baldassarre Valenti,
who cherished life, people and good books.

⟨ 1 ⟩

A Fine Place to Live

HIGH IN THE Alpine region of Austria is the small village of Gartendorf, nestled among snow-covered mountain peaks that seem to come alive when the snows of Advent begin to fall. Sometimes the snows approach suddenly from behind a mountain crest, blowing all around half of the village while the other half sits untouched in the gleaming sun. At other times the snows fall soft and silent over the whole village, covering fields and farms in a hushed blanket of white. At these times the sound of cowbells becomes distant and muffled, and the smell of snow hangs clear in the wintry air. After the snowfall, the Tyrolean peaks loom into the deepest blue sky, and as the sun

1

moves through the day, the shadows of clouds make it seem as if the mountains are moving.

It is a fine place to live, so close to the city where every day there is something new to see. Nicole Kinders always enjoyed the drive down to Innsbruck in the back of Mama's or Papa's car. She was eleven, with green eyes and long flowing hair the color of honey. She liked to see the city within the Alps, and especially liked the cathedral of Saint Jakob, the hotels and famous buildings where Papa played his trumpet in the Gartendorf Brass Band, and the rainbow colored houses that stood all in a row along the river. The only time she had not been happy to go was the first day of school a year ago, when she moved up from the elementary school in Gartendorf to the secondary school, or Hauptschule, in Innsbruck. It was a much bigger school, and it took a few days to grow accustomed to it. This year had been her sister Ashley's turn to be introduced to the new school, and she seemed to dance through the door on opening day, completely happy with the change.

Normally Nicole would be taking the tram with her sister, but today Papa was driving into the city for business, and the trip was much nicer by car. All the way into Innsbruck, Nicole could see signs of people dressing up their shops and houses for the winter festivities.

"Did you remember your lunch today?" Nicole asked.

Ashley held up her school sack with a big grin. She had lost a tooth two days ago, and there was a gap in her smile. "My hand warmer packet, too," she said.

"What for?"

"For just in case. It is winter, you know."

Papa drove twice around the Old Town block where the Zimt & Zucker bakery shop stood beckoning the early morning crowd. Nicole thought he forgot his way again, since he seemed to grow absent-minded sometimes when he was driving. But this time he stopped the car and turned to her. "They're starting the Christmas baking now, can you smell the cinnamon?"

"And some chocolate, too," she said.

"Can we buy a sweet?" Ashley begged with her hand outstretched over the back seat.

"Tell you what," Papa said. "Take two euros and buy a sweet for each of you. Now hurry along, you still have to walk over the bridge."

"Thank you, Papa," Nicole said as both girls blew kisses to him, and waved as he drove away.

"I'm freezing already," Ashley said. She was wearing her crazy ski hat with colored springs popping out all over, and she pulled it tight around her ears. She stopped walking and zipped her coat all the way to her chin. The wind whipped some leaves up off the ground and swirled them around in an icy gust. "Wow, Nicole — did you see that?"

The wind almost took Nicole's breath away, and

she could feel her eyes tear. "It's like a mini tornado," she said. When she wiped her eyes she noticed that the tram carrying the students from Gartendorf had just passed by, and was about to cross over the bridge toward school. "Let's not go in the bakery," she said.

"But — why not?"

"Because."

"That's a dumb answer. I want to get a Linzer piggy."

"Maybe after school," Nicole said. "Come — let's get going before we're late."

❀

IT TOOK ALL their strength to cross the bridge in the cutting wind. The river was especially blue, and ice was collecting at the edges. On the far side of the bridge was a familiar wooden market stall, painted with festive colors like a carousel. Today the canvas flaps were tied tight against the wind. Boznik, the shopkeeper, was a pleasant fellow with a big, crooked smile and thick, wavy brown hair, and two earrings in each ear. He had a pointed chin beard and twinkling eyes that made him look very much like an elf. "Good morning!" he said. He did not seem to mind the cold at all, and his jacket was open at his neck. He held three perfect red apples, and began to juggle them. "An apple for school?"

"Good morning," Nicole said, slowing down to watch. "No thanks — I have one. I'm not sure what I'd like." She peeked through the flaps of the market stall.

Ashley grabbed Nicole's arm and pulled. "I thought you said we have to hurry."

"Today we have a special new selection," Boznik said, putting the apples into a basket of assorted fruits. "Would you like to see?"

"We can't," Ashley said. "Maybe after school."

Nicole shook her arm free, and her school sack dropped partway down her shoulder. She hoisted it back up, and looked at Boznik. "My sister is mad at me because I wouldn't let her buy a Linzer pig at the bakery."

"I would be mad at you, too. But don't worry. Boznik the great confectioner can ease your woes!" He untied a flap of his stall and pulled it aside, and took out a cellophane packet. It was a Linzer pig, a cookie in the shape of a pig with a heart cutout and raspberry jam filling, dusted white with powdered sugar. "Is this what you had in mind?"

"How did you know?" Ashley said.

"Boznik knows his customers," he said. "That will be one euro for you."

"What about the new special selection?" asked Nicole. She looked at Boznik, and his eyes narrowed as he looked back at her. His face began to look mysterious, and his chin beard ruffled in the wind. She could hear Ashley open the cellophane and take a crunchy bite of her cookie.

Boznik reached into his stall and rummaged around. His back was turned long enough that Nicole began to grow impatient. She could feel her heart beating, partly from anticipation and partly from the fear of being late. She was just about to tell Boznik it was time to leave when he suddenly spun forward and waved a candy cane in the air like a wand. "This, my dear girl, is a magic candy cane!"

Nicole studied him to see if he was trying to make a joke. Sometimes Papa would tease her with a serious face, but he usually gave it away when he broke into a smile. Boznik did not smile. He looked straight into Nicole's eyes. "A magic candy cane," he said again.

"Magic?" she said. "What can it do?"

"Alas, if I could begin to tell you it would take half the day," he said.

"Thanks, but we're going to be late," Nicole said.

"We need to go," Ashley said. She wrapped the remaining half of her cookie and tucked it into her school sack. She had powdered sugar on her lips and gloves.

Boznik held his hand up, and in the palm was a tattoo of the ancient Aztec sun. "You should have this candy cane," he said. "The magic will be revealed."

"Thanks, but I'll save my money for later," Nicole said.

Boznik held out the candy cane in front of her. "Please take it. If you like it, you can come back later and pay me. If you don't like it, then you shall not have to pay me."

Nicole looked at the candy cane. It did not look magic, or even special in any way. It looked like an ordinary candy cane, maybe a little brighter red on the stripes, maybe a more luminous white, but that could just be an illusion caused by the clear wrapping or the cold wind in her eyes. Very gingerly, she reached for the candy cane. "How much?"

"Half a euro, but pay me later," Boznik said. "Now off to school with you!"

The school bell was ringing just as they arrived.

❨ 2 ❩

The Candy Cane

ALL MORNING NICOLE felt bored, fidgety — and she just couldn't find a way to calm down. In mathematics class she became overheated, and realized that she wasn't feeling well. She put her hand to her forehead, and felt cool sweat at her hairline. She shivered. Mr. Ziller was diagramming triangles on the board and explaining the differences between equilateral and isosceles triangles, and when he finished he turned to the class with his trademark question. "Clear as mud?"

Max Brunheim sat next to Nicole. He was a neighbor, the youngest of four brothers who lived on the Brunheim Farm about a half kilometer from her. Max had a mop of glossy, dark hair and a talent for mimicking teachers. His impersonation of Mr. Ziller would send Nicole into spasms of laughter. Max would make circles over his eyes and squint, and lift up and down on his toes and say, "Clear as mud? Clear as mud?" Of course he would never perform anywhere a teacher might see him, but sometimes in class he would turn to Nicole and arch his dark eyebrows while twisting his lips or flexing his nose, and Nicole would have to press her mouth closed to keep from laughing. He turned to her with a gleam in his eye that quickly dimmed and became a frown.

Nicole was breathing fast, and she felt weak. Her head felt very heavy, and she put it down on the desk to rest.

"Mr. Ziller, I think Nicole is sick," Max said.

"I see," he said, hurrying down the aisle. "Can you lift your head, Nicole?"

She lifted her head slowly. "I think I need to see the nurse."

The nurse was very tall and had short, chestnut hair. She always wore a lavender smock and a badge that said "School Nurse" on it. She helped Nicole up onto the examination table. She stretched the thermometer from its place on the wall like an old telephone, put a new cover on it, then gently probed into Nicole's ear. "Hmmm. Normal temperature," she said. "Does anything hurt you today?"

"I don't think so. I just don't feel well."

"Are you thinking about something? Is something making you feel worried or anxious?"

"Well...sort of. This may sound kind of lame."

"It can't be lame if it's important to you," the nurse said.

Nicole took a deep breath. "Is there really such a thing as magic? I mean, real magic. Not like Harry Potter or things like that."

The nurse's face lit up with concern. "That seems like a very big question," she said. "I would say there could be such a thing. What do you think?"

"I'm not sure." Nicole was about to tell the nurse all about Boznik the shopkeeper, and about the candy cane. But something stopped the words in her throat, and she began to shiver again.

The nurse took a blanket and wrapped it around Nicole's shoulders. "Maybe we can talk about it," she said. "Magic — that's when something happens all by itself that seems to go against the natural order. Like if I waved my hand and said, "Nicole Kinders is now going to feel wonderful!"

Nicole smiled. "It would be nice if that could make me feel better."

"But there are other kinds of magic, don't you see? For example — when your mama takes milk and cocoa and puts them together on the stove, and you get hot chocolate."

"That's not magic, it's just natural results."

"What about the aroma in the air, and the feeling you get when you're watching the little marshmallows melt on top? And the warm feeling when you test your first sip?"

"So it's not like making something float in the air?"

"I can't say I know much about that kind of magic," the nurse said. "I suppose it can happen, but I've never really seen it except in the movies."

"So if somebody tells you that something is magic, how could you find out?"

"Well — I suppose you have to experience it for yourself."

"How will I know?"

The nurse took Nicole's hand and helped her down from the table. "Oh, I think you'll just know. Some people think love is magic, others think money is magic. And there are some who think a talking horse would be magic."

Nicole smiled. "Max Brunheim said his father's horse can talk, but it only says, 'Ni—coooooole'."

The nurse laughed. "He certainly has a fresh sense of humor," she said. "Now I'm going to ask you to sit on this chair for a minute. I think the winter air made you a little dehydrated. I'm going to get you some water to drink before you go back to class."

BY THE TIME school was over for the day, Nicole had forgotten her queasiness. She joined her sister and

Max, along with a dozen other students waiting for the tram back to Gartendorf. From behind, she felt a hand swish up and down the sleeve of her coat, making a whistling sound. She pulled her arm away and glanced over her shoulder to see Max tugging his hand behind his back with a mischievous look on his face. "Go away," she said.

"Nice ski coat," Max said. "For space exploration, that is."

"Ha ha, Max," she said.

"Oh, chuckle chuckle," Ashley said. "Look how hard I'm laughing."

Max reached out to Ashley's ski hat and ruffled the multicolored springs that decorated the top and sides. "I wasn't talking to you, Ashley. Watch out, your brains are popping out of your head."

"Then I guess you better go wash your hands off," she said. Max looked at his hand and made a sour face as the tram came to a stop in front of them.

The driver, Mr. Engle, had an enormous moustache that curled at the ends. Nicole could smell peppermint when she climbed aboard, and she saw that Mr. Engle was sucking on a candy cane. Easy for him! That could not possibly be a magic candy cane — could it be? She was watching him to see if anything unusual might happen.

Somebody was speaking to her, but she hadn't been paying attention. "Hey, you're taking up two seats. Can you please put your stuff on the floor?"

She blinked her eyes and looked up to see Isabelle Schubert standing over her, trying to hold on as the tram started off with an electric whirring sound. Isabelle was the smartest girl in the class, and could play elaborate pieces on the piano with her eyes closed. "Oh, sorry," Nicole said. She grabbed her school sack and put it on the floor in front of her, wondering when it might be the right time to take out her candy cane. It would seem almost perfect right now, since Mr. Engle was working on his own candy cane with great relish.

"Are you okay?" Isabelle asked. "You looked like you were going to throw up in Mr. Ziller's class."

"Me? No, I'm okay," Nicole said. "I think I was just a little overheated. The nurse made me drink a lot of water."

"We were worried about you — especially Maximillian," she said, exaggerating each syllable of Max's full name. "Poor boy. He asked Mr. Ziller twice if he could go to the nurse and see if you were okay."

"Are you talking about me, Isabelle Schubert?" Max said from three seats away. "You're such a busybody, why don't you just go play the piano with your mouth shut instead of your eyes?"

Isabelle stood up with fire in her eyes, her blonde ponytail swishing behind her shoulder. "And why don't you just go milk a cow with your mouth instead of your hands?" she yelled to Max. She accidentally kicked Nicole's school sack over, and the top curled open just enough for the wrapped candy cane to skid out on the floor. Several students on the tram were looking at Max and laughing.

Nicole instantly reached for the candy cane, fearing the worst if it broke. She grabbed it up and held it in both hands as the tram lurched to a sudden halt. She could see that Max's face was red, and she wanted to tell everybody to hush up. Isabelle dropped hard into her seat. Mr. Engle plucked his candy cane from his mouth and said, "Please remain seated at all times for safety!"

Nicole began to realize that her hands were holding a broken candy cane. She looked at it, wondering if something terrible was going to happen.

The candy cane was only broken at the bottom, which could be a good chance for Nicole to have a taste of some and still save the rest. She tried to be nonchalant as she eased the broken piece from the wrapper, hoping that nobody would notice her fingers trembling. She glanced across the aisle at Ashley, who was joyfully ignoring everybody as she finished off her Linzer pig cookie.

Nothing happened. No thunder or wild animal stampede, no shattering pixelation of the entire tram and everybody in it — just a little spat between schoolmates.

The tram from Innsbruck to Gartendorf took only about ten minutes, long enough for the afternoon sun to dip behind the snowcapped mountains. Mr. Engle was crunching on the end of his candy cane as he brought the tram to a stop. "All right, everybody. Have a good night and come again tomorrow."

Nicole lifted her school sack and followed Isabelle out of the tram. Suddenly Max pushed his way between them and stood before Isabelle with his face menacingly close and his hands rolled into fists. Nicole could see a great fear growing on Isabelle's face. Max said, "You know what you said about me milking a cow?"

Isabelle took a step backward, a whimpering sound rising in her throat.

"Well, I think I might try it some time," he continued. "And then spit it out all over you."

"Stop it!" The command was strong and loud in the air, and Nicole realized that it came out of her mouth. "Just stop it. We're supposed to be friends."

Max turned to Nicole with a stare that made her stomach cold. "I'm going home," he said. "I have stuff to do."

❦

NICOLE'S FINGERS WERE sticky from holding the piece of candy cane, which she had somehow forgotten about until her hands began to freeze. She was a little puzzled with herself, because she had never been one to get involved in a fight. Maybe it was Max's uncustomary anger, or the terrified look on Isabelle's face that made Nicole speak up. Or maybe it could be the magic? She thought of Boznik and his sun tattoo, standing before her in the Alpine wind with the candy cane in his hand. "The magic will be revealed," he said. She was not sure what that meant, but it was time to find out.

The taste of her cold fingers plus the rush of peppermint flooded her senses. It was as if all the most wonderful flavors in her memory could be tasted at once. Instantly she could taste warm stew, and the garden vegetables that she would pick herself, and fresh purple grapes that came from her grandma's vine, and lemon ice that cooled her on the hottest summer day. She could smell the snow that the breezes blew in puffs off the trees, gleaming like diamond dust as it settled to the ground. The Gartendorf Mountains glistened pink in the setting sun, and the sky seemed a more brilliant hue than she had ever noticed before. She watched as a flock of tiny birds danced against the sky like confetti, then suddenly disappeared as they all turned sideways, only to reappear in a different place like fireworks.

Maybe there was magic in that candy cane, Nicole thought as she put on her gloves and continued her walk with Ashley. So far it was good magic. How long would it last? And would there be any black magic? And how could she tell which things came from the candy cane and which things came from inside herself?

"You smell like peppermint," Ashley said.

"Do you like it?"

"It's okay. Reminds me of Christmas. Mama said we're going to get the Christmas tree on Saturday."

"Remember last year when we all went in Papa's car to get the Christmas tree, and Papa got lost trying to find his way out of the tree farm?" Nicole said. "And then when we were coming home, the tree blew off the top of the car?"

"Oh my gosh," Ashley laughed. "Mama was yelling, 'Stop the car, Friedrich! Stop the car!' Then Papa got out and ran to fetch the tree, and he was all mad because he thought he was going to be late for concert practice."

"Oh, and remember?" Nicole said. "After we got the tree home, he stood outside with his trumpet, and he played 'Good King Wenceslas' until Mr. Brunheim came to pick him up."

"I wonder if anything so strange is going to happen this year," Ashley said.

❧ 3 ❧

Scrambled Magic

SATURDAY COULD NOT come fast enough. Nicole woke up at the crack of first light and hurried into the bathroom. She noticed that Mama had set out towels decorated with holly designs. Looking out the window, she could see that it had snowed overnight. A squirrel was sitting on top of a fence post, looking like a strange Russian hat. Somehow she still felt magic from two days ago, and she hadn't touched the rest of her candy cane yet.

She tiptoed back into her room and got dressed as fast as she could. The morning would be busy with chores, and after breakfast would be her karate class, Ashley's dance class, Papa's brass band practice, and Mama's real estate appointment with an American who wanted to buy a chalet. Mama spoke very good English because she had lived in Boston for two years while she attended college. She said the American was a doctor who would be working in Innsbruck, and had many skiing friends that would come for vacations.

Across the hall, Ashley opened her door and lumbered out in ski pants, pulling her crazy ski hat on. "Did you see the snow? We should go skiing," she said, the springs on her ski hat bouncing.

"Now?" Nicole said. "We have to make our beds and clean our rooms."

"You're so bossy. Let's just go out now."

"Ashley, you're such a troublemaker." Nicole hastily arranged her quilt across her bed and fluffed up the pillow. "If Mama finds out —"

"She's upstairs sleeping," Ashley said. "Who says she's going to know?"

"You have a hole in your sock."

"So what? Let's just go."

Nicole found her ski pants and fleece hat, and followed Ashley to the back door where they quietly put on their cross-country boots. When they opened the door, there was a snowdrift that was almost to their knees. Nicole put on her gloves and brushed away the drift. "It's perfect snow," she said.

"You're getting it all over the floor," Ashley said.

"So sweep it out if you're so worried."

"Never mind, let's just go."

They crossed the back porch to the ski rack and

lifted out their skis. Once they were on the snow, they snapped on the skis and began crossing the great field that stretched for about a kilometer along the Brunheim Farm road. They had no tracks to follow, but glided along easily because the new snow was just ankle-deep. Nicole loved the pressing sound it made beneath their skis. The air was clear and sweet, not too cold, with a slight smell of cows. Usually the breezes carried the farm smell in the opposite direction, into the hiking trails and the mountains, but sometimes it would drift into the village.

The girls flew along side by side for a while, but Nicole was somewhat taller and found herself having to slow down to keep together with Ashley. She was getting thirsty, so she stopped to eat some snow and let Ashley get ahead. The first mouthful of snow melted fast, the second chilled her teeth. She looked up to see Ashley forging ahead. She grabbed one more bunch of snow and tossed it in her mouth, getting some down her neck, then she hustled along to catch up.

Just as they were passing the farm, the Brunheims' Austrian Pinscher came barking toward them from the crest of the hill. His name was Blitzen, but the girls called him Fang because he once bit Ashley and was known to bite people now and then. Mr. Brunheim was told by the animal control officer that he had to install an electric dog fence to keep Blitzen from bothering skiers and hikers on the trails.

"Go home, Fang! Go home!" Nicole yelled. The

dog sprang ahead a few more steps and suddenly stopped in a flash of dog and snow, let out a loud yelp and turned completely around, galloping back out of sight toward the farm.

"I hate that dog," Ashley said.

"Don't worry, I think he hit the fence," Nicole said as she picked up her pace again. She thought she heard the sound of a twig snapping, then a sudden rush of air and color whizzed in front of her face. She lurched to a stop so quickly she lost her balance and almost fell over. Was that a bird she saw?

Ashley stopped skiing and spun around. "Hey — what are you doing?"

"Something almost hit me." Nicole looked around, but whatever flew by had buried itself in the snow. She looked up to see if something had fallen from a tree, but there were no branches directly above. Then in flew another object, and another, landing just a little way from them. As she was bending over to adjust her ski pants, she heard a cracking sound and then distant laughter that sounded like boys or men.

Then, WHAM! The shock of pain caused her to cry out. "Oww — oww!" She couldn't tell where she was hit, but there was a stunning, paralyzing pain radiating throughout her lower body. Tears sprang to her eyes as her left leg began to buckle beneath her. She frantically tried to stay standing, but felt herself collapsing and saw the ground rushing up at her face. She landed hard in the snow. She quickly realized that the impact was on her behind, directly where muscle and bone met at the pelvis. Fretful that it might be a gunshot, she looked down to see if her ski pants had a hole. "Ashley, I'm hurt. I'm hurt a lot."

"Oh my gosh, it's golf balls!" Ashley shouted. She skied back and stood over Nicole.

"Golf balls?" Nicole barely said the words when two more round missiles pelted the snow nearby.

Ashley picked a blue golf ball out of its hole in the snow. "Those ones they use at the mini golf place," she said.

"Let's get out of here!" Nicole said. "If they hit us in the head we'll be killed."

"Can you get up?" Ashley dropped the ball and leaned over to help Nicole lift herself.

"I think so," Nicole said. "Cover your head!" She could see that somebody was firing multicolored golf balls at them, two and three at a time, but she could not see who was doing it beyond the crest of the hill.

They scrambled as fast as they could to get away from the Brunheim Farm. She suspected that it must have been Max and his obnoxious older brother Andreas, and maybe even their next brother Stefan, who had been in trouble with the police. They were the only ones who lived on that land, and it was unlikely their parents would be standing in the snow to drive golf balls toward open hiking trails. She hustled along, trying to keep up with Ashley while her whole left leg was cramping. Snow was melting down her face, and she could feel her insides boiling with fear and anger. They were doing this on purpose, and laughing about it! She wanted to ski directly to the farm and bang each one of them over the head with a golf ball. So much for sitting next to Max in school. If there was any magic in that candy cane, she wished it would let her torch his hair with one look of her eyes!

Soon they were in sight of home, speeding along the same tracks they had made on the way out. "Hey, Ashley?"

"What."

"Let's not say anything, okay? Promise me you won't tell."

"We didn't do anything wrong. Papa should go over there and speak with —"

"Just hush yourself," she said, then whispered, "Mama might hear you."

"So she's going to see we went skiing anyway." Ashley stopped at the back porch and took off her skis.

"I'm not talking about that. If Papa finds out about the golf balls, he'll go over there. They have guns."

"They do not," Ashley said. "You're just making that up."

"I am not! Last summer I saw Mr. Brunheim shoot a bunny rabbit, and Fang ran to fetch it and brought it back in his mouth."

"Did not," Ashley said, crossing both hands in front of her throat. "Did he really?"

"Don't go crying about it, that's how come I didn't

tell you before. Now let's just go inside and act completely normal." She took off her skis and hung them back on the rack. She was not feeling the least bit of magic now, only a pounding heart and a pain that surged halfway down her leg. Once inside, she took the broom and dusted snow off the threshold, then closed the door.

"We shouldn't have gone," Ashley said. She pulled off her cross-country boots and crazy hat, and her curly blonde hair followed the hat up in a pulse of static electricity. "What time is it?"

"It's twenty past eight. We better wake Mama up, our classes start at ten." Nicole limped to her room. She slowly took off her ski pants and inspected the damage. "Great, now I have a big bruise on my butt."

"It looks really bad, Nicole. Does it hurt a lot?"

"It kills," she said, touching gently with a finger. "Owww! Why would anybody do such a thing?"

"I'm going to wake up Mama," Ashley said.

"Don't you dare say a word."

While Ashley was gone Nicole changed into her karate outfit and went into the kitchen, doing her best not to limp. She took out a saucepan and filled it halfway with milk, then put it on the stove. There were three things Nicole could make by herself: hot chocolate, pancakes and scrambled eggs. Papa sometimes teased her that she was going to make chocolate eggs and scrambled pancakes.

She was mixing the hot chocolate when Papa came into the kitchen. "How is my sweetness?" he said.

"Good morning, Papa." She reached her arms around his neck and kissed him. "You need to shave."

"Ah yes — that will come in time for the Christmas concert tonight," he said. "Do you want me to make you some breakfast?"

"What shall we have?"

"I received a wonderful surprise yesterday from Italy," he said, taking a large bundle from the bread keeper. "This is a panettone, straight from our business associates in Benevento." He opened the bundle to reveal a tall round bread that smelled lightly sweet with a hint of citron. He drew a long bread knife from its holder and cut a big slice out of the loaf and laid it on a plate.

Ashley came dancing into the kitchen. "Papa! Can we just skip our classes today and go directly to get our Christmas tree?"

"Absolutely not, my sweetness. Mama and I have important business this morning, and there will be plenty of time for that later. Now come and have some breakfast."

"I made some hot chocolate for you," Nicole said. She brought two cups to the table and placed one in front of Ashley. "Now be careful, it's very hot." She began to sit down and landed directly on her bruise, gasping aloud.

"Something wrong?" Papa said as he prepared coffee.

"I — I think I just sat wrong." She shifted in her seat to take the weight off her bruise. "Hey, this bread is really good," she said, trying to change the subject. "What do they call it?"

"That's panettone," he said absentmindedly as he took out his phone and began scrolling up and down with his thumb, looking at the screen. "It was a gift."

"Hey Papa," Ashley said. "We went skiing this morning."

"Is that so?" he said, still looking at his phone. He put it to his ear and waited.

"We went almost all the way to the farm, and we —"

Nicole kicked her under the table.

"Owwww!"

"Just eat your breakfast, girls," Papa said. He stepped out of the kitchen and they could hear him speaking on the phone.

Nicole stared daggers at Ashley, who was pouting with her arms folded in front of her. "Just don't say anything about it, okay?"

"For your information, I wasn't going to."

"Well, you came terribly close, so hush yourself."

❧ 4 ❧

O Tannenbaum

THE KARATE CLASS was one step below horrible.

Although it could have been even worse. At least the Brunheim boys were not enrolled. Nicole couldn't imagine why her neighbors would do such an outrageous thing. Lately Max seemed to be under the control of some dark force. She dreaded seeing him at school Monday. She expected to ask him who was driving golf balls from the farm at her and Ashley, but she didn't know how he might react. What if he made fists like he did with Isabelle Schubert? Or worse? The thought of it made her insides creep.

Nicole tried stretching out her leg and flexing her back, but there was no getting out of it. She had a bruise that was going to keep barking at her all day, maybe longer. Kicks and spins, thrusts and cartwheel exercises all joined together to give her a concert of pain. She was trying her very best to be the ultimate karate student, to ignore the pain and focus, focus, focus! But by the time class was over, she was just trying her best not to limp.

"Okay, wonderful karate students," Sensei Krafft said. "We have one more class before Christmas break. Please remember to practice!"

Nicole found her coat and walked outside the karate school, expecting to see Mama's car. She knew that sometimes real estate appointments ran longer than expected. That could mean the visitors were going to buy a house, which was excellent. Then she remembered Mama telling her she would have to walk over to Ashley's dance school and wait with her there.

Somehow walking was not as painful as she feared. Once she started, it seemed the ordinary motion calmed the pain. By the time she turned the corner onto Lindenstrasse, she could see that Mama still had not arrived. No forest green car, no sign of any dance students. She walked to the front entrance of the dance school and was just about to pull open the glass door when Ashley appeared on the other side. Ashley pushed the door open with both hands.

"Hey Nicole, we have to wait for about a half hour. Mama called the school and said she was running late."

"Is she selling the chalet?"

"I don't know."

They waited together until the cold got to be too much, then they walked across the street to a lunch shop. "I have one euro, that's enough to get a gingerbread man," Nicole said.

Suddenly the car appeared at the end of the street. "Wait, there she is!" Ashley said. She clutched Nicole's coat sleeve and pulled her away from the lunch shop door. They both ran up the street, Ashley reaching the car first. She pulled the back door open almost into Nicole.

"Ashley, you're going to smack me," she said. "Hi Mama! Where's Papa?"

"Is something wrong with your leg, Nicole?" Mama said.

"I think I have a little cramp from karate."

"Yeah, she has a cramp in her butt," Ashley said.

"You'll probably need a little more potassium in your diet," Mama said. "We have fresh bananas at home."

"Where's Papa?" Nicole asked, pulling on her seat belt. "Ashley, get your belt on."

"That's why I'm late, sweetie. Mr. Brunheim called at the last minute to say he couldn't come today for rehearsal. One of the boys had an accident or something. Papa took his own car."

Nicole stiffened, feeling a sudden flush in her cheeks. One of the boys had an accident? She wondered which one, and how? Probably slipped on a golf ball — or got whacked in the head by the brother's golf club. That would serve him right, she thought.

"So how will we get the Christmas tree?" Ashley said.

"Ashley, you're whining. We're going to go home first and meet Papa there, and Nicole, you can change into something a little warmer. Then we'll go have a nice lunch before we go to the tree farm."

"Yayyy!!" they both clapped.

"Mama, you know that boy Anheuser in my school?" Ashley said. "He said that you're not supposed to put up a tree until Christmas Eve. He said it's wrong to put it up so early when people should be celebrating Saint Nicholas."

"Oh, I don't think people should get bossy about how other people choose to celebrate," she said. "Some people wait till Christmas Eve to decorate their tree, and others decorate before."

"What was Christmas like when you were little?" Ashley asked.

"Well, Grandma is very traditional. We would never see our Christmas tree until after dinner Christmas Eve. Uncle Johan and Aunt Valeria and I would be so excited that we barely touched our fried fish. We kept looking at the closed door to the living room, thinking about Kristkindl, the Christ child, being in our own home. And when we heard the magic chimes, we just about tumbled through the door to see the beautiful tree all lit up and decorated with goodies and presents! And underneath it would be my grandfather's hand carved manger scene with Baby Jesus sleeping on the straw that we three kids put there piece by piece with our good deeds. We would sing, and my Papa would go out the front door and write with a piece of chalk on the doorway, CMB."

"I know what that is," Nicole said. "That's the initials of the Three Wise Men — Caspar, Melchior and Balthazar."

"That's absolutely right," Mama said. "Did Grandpa teach you that?"

"I think it was Grandma."

"That was originally a farm tradition, to have the Wise Men protect the farm and herds through the year. Then my Papa would come in and read from the Nativity in the Bible, and we would open all our presents."

"We still do most of that," Nicole said. "Except I think it's much nicer to decorate all together instead of waiting."

"Yes, your Papa and I thought we would have our own traditions, and it seems like plenty of other people do, too."

❡ ✳ ❡

THE TREE FARM was hopping with activity. Dozens of cars were in the lot, some with snow still on the roof.

A group of handbell ringers from the high school bell chorus was greeting people with "Oh Tannenbaum." A large outdoor fireplace was blazing with cut off branches and tree bottoms, and the air was rich with the heady aromas of pine and hot apple cider. The tree workers were all dressed in Alpine hats and leather aprons, helping customers to select the perfect tree, shake off the snow, trim the bottom, and tie the tree onto their car. There was a cashier stall with lights and tree stands, and nearby stood Saint Nicholas and Krampus handing out free hot cider. Krampus was dressed in a devilish outfit of fur with horns on his head and chains hanging all about, and really looked as if he could tell which children would be getting sticks and switches in their shoes. Saint Nicholas had a white beard, and wore a long golden robe with white fur lining, and a bishop's mitre on his head.

As much as Nicole was enjoying the tree farm, she was restless, eager to get home with the Christmas tree so that they could at least string the lights on today. Ashley had wandered over to the cashier stall to talk with Saint Nicholas, and who knew how long that would last? Ashley seemed to be so much more sociable than Nicole. Saint Nicholas ladled out a cup of cider for Ashley, and from where Nicole stood, she could hear their conversation.

"Is Saint Nicholas really real?" Ashley asked.

"As I stand before you!" he smiled, and put a white

gloved hand on Ashley's shoulder. "I am merely a messenger. Our beloved Saint Nicholas is a living spirit, and that means he can take earthly form any way he likes. He is Santa Claus in America, Father Christmas in Britain, Saint Nicholas here as you know — and he can possess any person on earth with generosity and good cheer. If you're open to his presence, you can feel it."

Nicole walked over to the stand, and Krampus came forward to hand her a cup of cider. "By the Man in the Moon!" he growled. "Here we have a naughty child."

Nicole giggled. "No, I'm not. That's not true."

"Well then, perhaps you'll need a test," he said, stamping his feet and making his chains rattle.

"Maybe you should test Papa," she said, sipping on the cider. "He put out his shoe for goodies one time, and he got a bundle of switches instead."

"So you see! Nobody can fool old Krampus," he said. "Do you know your prayers, young lady?"

"Most of them," she said quickly, knowing the test all too well. If Krampus caught you slacking, he'd chase you with his switch, and you would have to run to Saint Nicholas for protection.

"Do you know your lessons?" Krampus growled.

"Yes, most of them."

"Can you sing a song?"

"I can sing 'Silent Night' in German and in English."

"And how many months have twenty-eight days?"

Nicole was about to say February, but saw Krampus beginning to lift his switch. She hesitated, then said, "All of them!"

Krampus rattled his chains and stamped on the ground. "By the Man in the Moon! I'll have to look elsewhere for a naughty child."

Nicole moved closer to Ashley, who was still talking with Saint Nicholas. "My Papa plays the trumpet. Does Saint Nicholas play a musical instrument?"

He stroked his beard. "Sometimes Saint Nicholas will play on a pennywhistle, other times a trombone — and sometimes he plays rock and roll on a guitar!"

Nicole looked ahead to discover a news camera trained on them from a few meters away. Nearby stood Mama with the most abundant fir tree Nicole had ever seen. A rush of excitement overcame her. She placed her half-finished cider cup on the cashier stall and hurried over to her mother. "Where's Papa?" she asked.

"He's exploring the back lot, looking for a wreath," she said.

A newswoman stepped over with her microphone. "Good day, madam," she said. "Are you this girl's mother?"

"Yes, I am."

"Madam, we have some wonderful footage of your daughter, and we'd like permission to have this on the news."

"I believe you have both my daughters in there," she smiled. "This one is Nicole Kinders, and her sister is named Ashley. She's the one with the curly blonde hair talking with Saint Nicholas. Sure, we'll give our permission."

"Thank you, madam, and thank you, Nicole Kinders," she said.

"You're very welcome," Mama said.

Nicole spread her arms out and ruffled the boughs of the tree. It would be just the perfect size for their parlor, standing tall in the picture window at the front of their house. "Papa will have to tie it on the car especially well," she said.

"You think so?" Mama winked. Her phone began ringing with Papa's ringtone, and she took it out of her coat, looked at the screen, and put it to her ear. "Yes, honey?"

Nicole could hear his voice from the phone. "This place is like a maze, where are you?"

"I'm near the cashier stall. Follow your nose to the fireplace."

"I already did that twice, and ended up behind the fence."

"Try one more time, you'll make it."

Papa finally found his way to the stall. Nicole and Ashley both rushed over and surrounded him, talking at the same time. "We're going to be on the news! You should smell the Christmas tree! Can we hurry up?"

"Yes, my darlings — we will hurry home. Will you

please hold this wreath while I help Mama carry the tree to the car?"

ON THE WAY HOME, Nicole held on tight to one of the ropes that secured the tree. The rope was wedged by the closed door, but she really wanted to make sure this time that the tree wouldn't blow off. She asked, "Papa? Did you ever hear about snow that fell all at once?"

"What do you mean, like an avalanche? Or off a roof?"

"No. Like if you could ever get fifteen or twenty centimeters that all came down at once, instead of snowflakes."

"Now that's an interesting question," Papa said. "I'm so glad you asked it, because just last week I spoke with Professor Nikolai Nikolosantapopov at the University of Siberia. He told me that sort of thing can happen in certain parts of the Ural Mountains."

"Really?"

"Well, there was a college girl from America who was traveling the world in her studies about snow. She was doing a thesis on the taste of snow in different regions, and if there was any health benefit to eating the snow of France or Italy or Austria, as compared to China or America."

"Isn't all snow from the same sky?" Mama said, turning to Papa and batting her eyes.

"Well, yes," Papa said, "but aren't all people from the same heaven? When snow falls, it is subject to all the influences of the surrounding air. For example, snow falling through the mountain winds in Switzerland can have a sweet taste with a hint of chocolate."

"Chocolate snow?" Ashley giggled. "Wouldn't it be brown?"

"It's white chocolate," Papa said.

"I think we have peppermint snow in Austria," Nicole said.

"Yes, yes — you know exactly what I'm talking about," Papa continued. "So this student was visiting Professor Nikolosantapopov's class just in time for a field trip to the forest of Perm. She —"

"What was her name?" Ashley said.

"The student's name? It was Virginia. Virginia Beach. And she was in Russia for some snow tasting. Professor Nikolosantapopov took the class to the deep forest of Perm in an old rust bucket school bus with six bald tires and a smoking clutch. They had clear roads all the way in, but there was a prediction for a light snowfall — which in Perm usually means twenty centimeters. So there they are waiting and waiting under a gray Russian sky, when FOOOMPH! Down from the sky comes the entire twenty centimeters all at once, like it just dropped from a rooftop."

"Did anybody get hurt?" Nicole asked, letting go of the rope and rubbing her hands together. She noticed she had rope marks on her left hand, so she switched to hold it with her right hand.

"Funny you should ask," Papa said. "Virginia was just about to step out of the bus when the snow came down."

"FOOOMPH!" Ashley said. "Just like that?"

"Just like that."

"Wait, Papa! It's a red light. Red light!"

"Friedrich, stop the car!" Mama cried, clutching the dashboard with both hands.

The car stopped just in time. "Sorry, sorry," Papa said.

Nicole and Ashley looked at each other across the back seat and broke into peals of laughter, and kept laughing until the light turned green.

"Yes," Papa continued. "Yes. And the snow that fell on top of the bus? Some of it went right into Virginia's mouth, and some went in the top of her shoes."

"Didn't she have boots?" Ashley asked.

"Of course, but she wasn't wearing them since there was no snow at the time. But everybody else was on the bus, and they were amazed at what they saw. Virginia was first to taste the new snow, and she thought it tasted like a tin pie plate."

"Without any pie?" Nicole asked.

"Well, to be precise, there was the residue of cabbage and potato peel, but only the vaguest hint."

"Yucky," Nicole said.

"Indeed," Papa said. "That was the end of Virginia's snow tasting study. Of course it took three days to get out of the Perm forest. The rust bucket of a school bus was burning oil, and the tires were frankfurter skins, so they had to get the college boys out to push a few times when the wheels were just spinning around and spattering mud and snow all over the place."

"Weren't they freezing?" Ashley asked.

"Oh you bet they were," Papa said. "The only reason they didn't all die out there in the cold — well, there were two reasons. One, they had the snow insulating the bus a little bit, not as good as an igloo, but still enough to give a little protection. And two, everybody huddled together at night to share their body heat. Professor Nikolosantapopov said that the people with the stinky feet got to sleep in the back of the bus."

"That would be you, Papa," Nicole said.

"Hey, I don't have stinky feet!" he said.

"Now I think we can do without the unnecessary details," Mama said.

"Papa?" Ashley asked.

"Yes?"

"Do people ever play golf in the snow?"

Nicole darted a look of alarm and warning at Ashley. She knew Ashley registered the look, because Ashley looked back for just an instant. "Ashley, leave Papa alone for now. Look, we're almost home."

"Shut up, Nicole."

"No, you shut up."

"Shut up yourself. I said shut up first," Ashley said.

"No, I said shut up first, only I didn't say it rudely."

"So I did say shut up first," Ashley said and folded her arms.

"I'm older than you, so I get to tell you to shut up," Nicole said. "So just *shut up*."

"Now girls," Mama said with her listen-or-else tone of voice. "You've been so good since Advent began. Do you want Baby Jesus to have plenty of straw in his manger from your good deeds, or do you want to leave him a hard and barren manger?"

"Sorry, Mama," Nicole said.

"Papa carved that manger from a birch log when he was just fourteen years old," Mama continued. "And each year you girls have filled it with more and more pieces of straw."

"We have, Mama," Ashley said. "And I wasn't intending to do anything bad, I was just asking Papa if he knows anybody who plays golf in the snow."

Nicole let go of the rope holding the Christmas tree and hit Ashley in the face. "Ashley, I HATE YOU! You're a terrible, bad sister and you know I asked you to be quiet and you just keep prattling on no matter what," she sputtered, and began crying.

Ashley's hands flew to cover her face, and her eyes were agape with horror that Nicole had actually struck her. When she lifted her hands away, there was blood on her lip.

The car was pulling up in front of the car port. "Girls, girls," Papa said quietly. "You're making me very sad with all this fighting. Nicole, that was completely unacceptable. You need to go to your room and stay there for one hour. I hope you will take a nap, because I think you're overtired. Ashley, you know I'm not fond of you girls saying shut up to one another."

"She shouldn't be trying to boss me!" she said.

"Do not interrupt me. Now to answer your question that you seem so curious about, the answer is no. I do not know anybody who plays golf in the snow. Now you will go to your room for one hour. And you also should take a nap. When you come out of your room, Mama and I will have the Christmas tree all set up in the stand for you to see. Now go."

Nicole stomped into the house and went straight to her room. She was just about to slam the door when she noticed her school sack in the corner with the candy cane poking out. She didn't remember moving the candy cane from inside the sack, but there it was as red and white as could be, as if it found its own way to the top. She knew she couldn't blame Ashley because she had been out with her all day.

She slumped onto her bed as Ashley came down the hall holding a wad of snow against her lip. Ashley was about to go into her room, but first turned to look in Nicole's open doorway. The snow was melting and dripping from Ashley's chin and hand. "You shouldn't have said that to me," she said, sniffling.

Nicole's eyes were overflowing, and she blinked back her tears. "I didn't mean to hurt you. You weren't supposed to speak about what happened today, and you just kept doing it."

"But Nicole, what am I supposed to do?" Ashley stepped into the room, and sat next to Nicole on the bed. "Those boys could have killed you, and they did it on purpose. We're just kids, and I'm really scared."

"I'm scared too. But it's Christmas time, and I don't want to start trouble with the Brunheims. Papa and Mr. Brunheim aren't really friends, but we buy eggs and meat from them, and they go to brass band practice together to save on fuel. So let's just wait until after Christmas and maybe we can talk to Papa then, okay?"

❄

WHEN NICOLE WOKE up she became aware that Ashley had fallen asleep next to her and was still sound asleep. There was a wet spot on the quilt from the melting snow Ashley had been using to soothe her fat lip. Nicole could hear Papa's voice from the parlor.

She yawned and stretched her arms and legs, suddenly feeling a twinge where the golf ball made its mark. It was just as painful as it had been, and it reminded her of what had happened. She took a long peek at the ugly bruise. It was no longer raised like a bottle cap, that much was good. She slipped out of bed and padded down the hallway, stopping before she arrived at the end so she could hear her parents talk without being detected. The scent of fresh pine was strong in the air.

"What was all the fuss about golfing in the snow?" she heard from her mother.

"It's my fault, Julia," said her father. "I think Ashley wanted me to make a story with her, like the one I was making with Nicole about the Russian snow. I feel bad about not picking up on Ashley's question."

"I don't know," her mother said. "Ashley seemed to be enjoying your story just fine."

"True. But maybe she was trying to engage me with a new idea, and I snubbed her."

"No, Friedrich — I think something else is going on. They never fight like that."

"Ashley does sometimes instigate," he said. "Nicole is starting to grow into a young woman, and you know how that can be."

"There's no excuse for bad behavior," she said.

Nicole hated being the subject of her parents' discussions, and now that they were talking about exactly what she was trying to keep from them, she could feel her stomach squirming. Perhaps if she had told them right away about the golf ball attack, she would not have to be worrying about it now. But then again, if she had told them, she knew her father would be off to the Brunheim Farm, and who knows how that would end up? Her father was a perfect gentleman unless provoked beyond his patience. She had seen him turn frightfully angry a couple of times, but she had also seen Mr. Brunheim shoot a rabbit dead with a gun.

She backed up silently until she was at her bedroom door. She tiptoed in and put her hand on Ashley's shoulder. "Come on, Ashley. Let's go see the Christmas tree."

❯ 5 ❮

The Golden Trumpet

THE BRASS BAND concert was to begin at 7:30. Papa had his trumpet case ready by the door with his Alpine hat, and Mama was hurrying to put dinner on the table. Nicole put out silverware on new Christmas napkins that she had received as a gift from one of the retirement home patients when she did volunteer work there as a Girl Guide. She sat down carefully, placing her napkin in her lap.

The oven timer began beeping at the same time Mama's phone rang. Nicole watched as Mama turned off the timer, grabbed a potholder and swung open the oven door, pulled out a bubbling hot noodle casserole and placed it in the center of the table, then looked at her telephone screen, pressed OK and said in English, "Good evening, Julia Kinders speaking," all as one continuous motion. Papa meanwhile had been at the refrigerator, bringing out milk and sparkling water. He poured milk into the girls' glasses, then put the milk down and stood still, watching Mama.

"Yes, Dr. Johnson," she said. "I understand. Would you be interested in something a little larger? I have a wonderful place in Innsbruck we can see tomorrow. Yes, right after noon would be perfect." She thumbed the screen off and tossed the phone onto the counter. "I can't believe the call actually came through. My battery is completely down," she said.

"Why don't you charge it now so —"

"We're having our dinner. No outside business," she said, sighing heavily as she sat down. "I really didn't want to be showing property tomorrow. I thought for sure he would like the chalet."

Papa reached over and held her hand across the table. "We will have fun anyway," he said. "Now let's say our blessing and have dinner."

❦

AS THEY DROVE to the concert hall, Papa said, "Did you hear about the magic trumpet boy?"

"Was that you, Papa?" Ashley said. "How old were you when you started to play?"

"I think I was Nicole's age, probably eleven or so. I can tell you that I was not the magic trumpet boy. I had to practice, practice, as much as I could. Most of the time I just sounded like a car horn."

"Really? Then how did you learn?"

"I had a wonderful teacher. He was a fellow named Mr. Bernard, and he talked exactly like Ludwig von Drake. He used to come after school and teach music to us. I loved the sound of a brass band playing, and so I asked my father if I could learn trumpet, and he bought me a golden trumpet.

"Now in lessons, Mr. Bernard would sit next to you and point to each note on the music stand with a pencil, and hum out the tune in time, and if you hit too many false notes he would stop and look at you over his eyeglasses. 'Did you practice this piece?' he would say with that von Drake voice. 'Hold out your hand, get your punishment.' And then he would give you this little gentle baby slap, just to let you know that you needed to practice a lot to master the instrument. He always said, 'It's not fun to practice. The fun begins once you know your instrument!' And he was right, because by the time I got to high school, I was good enough to play in the high school orchestra."

"Is Mr. Bernard still alive?" Nicole asked.

"Oh, he died when I was away at college," Papa said.

"That's too bad. So what about the magic trumpet boy?"

"Yes, yes — we were talking about him. Back in the bad times, there was a Jewish boy named Harold who lived in Vienna. Now in those times, the Gestapo was ordered to arrest Jewish people and take them away to prison camps. Harold lived with his father and mother and two sisters in a big apartment building. It was a very musical building. Twelve apartments, with Christian families and Jewish families. The people would visit one another and share recipes and music. On a summer day when windows were open, you would walk by and hear wonderful jazz and classical pieces, played by the oldest to the youngest.

"Now whenever word got around that the police would be coming to arrest Jews, the Christian families in that building would gather the Jewish children into their apartments and pretend they were their own. One by one the Jewish parents would be taken away, never to be heard from again. But whoever was able to dodge the Gestapo would keep playing the music.

"Harold had a special talent, and could play trumpet from five years old. When he played, he had a certain flair, a rhythm that just got you paying attention. Everybody called him the magic trumpet boy. He could get people dancing because he made that trumpet come alive.

"Well, one day the Gestapo arrested his father at work, and he never got to say goodbye to the family. Harold's two older sisters decided they all should flee to America. Inge and Helene made arrangements for them all to go, but their mother refused to leave. 'This is my home,' she said, 'and I will stay and wait for my husband to be released.' Harold was only fourteen, but he knew there would be no release for his father. The neighbors tried to make him go with his sisters. But he also refused to leave. 'Somebody has to stay and play the music,' Harold said."

"Did Inge and Helene make it to America?" Ashley asked.

"Yes, they did," he said. "They both got married and had children in Massachusetts."

"So what happened to Harold?" Nicole said.

"Well, he was able to dodge the enemy for almost two years, until somebody at his school let it slip that Harold was Jewish. A family member who worked for the Gestapo overheard. So they came and broke down Harold's door in the middle of the night and murdered his mother right in front of him. Then they stole all of the silverware, money, jewelry and his trumpet, and dragged him off to a prison camp."

"Friedrich? Friedrich, darling," Mama interrupted. "This is a terribly sad story to be telling children at Christmas time."

"It is a sad story, but —"

"Please don't tell it," she said.

"No, tell it!" Nicole said. "It's like when King Herod killed all those babies, and Mary and Joseph had to flee into Egypt. Please, we need to hear the rest. What happened to his trumpet? What happened to Harold?"

"Well, I'm getting to that part. The government

decided they could get free music by making the musical prisoners play. But Harold was brokenhearted now because he was an orphan and he knew he may never see his beautiful sisters ever, ever again. His spirit was so crushed that he almost didn't care to live anymore.

"Then one day another boy that used to live in his building turned up at the prison camp. 'Harold,' he said. 'The others are telling me that if we play music, the enemy will keep us alive to entertain them. We can show up at practice in the morning.' Then Harold said, 'I will entertain them by spitting in their coffee.'

"His friend said, 'Don't be a fool, we must stay alive. Life is short enough, and the bad times will end. Come with me tomorrow and we will play.' So the next morning, Harold went to the music building, and there among all the other stolen instruments was his trumpet! He picked it up and played on it, and everybody told him to make sure not to play jazz. You could only play approved music in those days. So everybody who had an instrument joined in and played their best.

"Now after the practice, Harold was cleaning his trumpet — and out dropped a gold ring. It was his mother's wedding ring, and he realized she had hidden it in the trumpet because she knew that musical instruments might have a chance to be protected from the scrap yard. He saw this as a sign from his mother to keep playing music, and he kept the ring hidden in the horn all through his time in the prison camp. When the war was over, Harold and his friend were both very skinny and sick, but they were alive. Harold met a wonderful girl and gave her his mother's ring, and you could just imagine the music that they played on that wedding day! Harold's friend said, 'you play that music because you're happy,' and Harold looked at him and said, 'No. I don't play the music because I'm happy. I am happy because I play the music.'"

"That's a cool story, Papa," Nicole said. "I'm really glad you told it."

"Yes, me too," Ashley said. "Did Harold have a last name?"

"Oh. Yes, indeed he did," Papa said. "His name was Harold Bernard, Mr. Bernard. And he became a famous trumpet player and music teacher. My music teacher."

❦ �֎ ❧

SOMEHOW NICOLE ENDED up with the best seat in the concert hall, right in the middle and a few rows back from the stage, with Mama on her left and Ashley on her right. She was reading her ticket, which said: "Musikkapelle Gartendorf, 7:30 PM December 3," when the curtain opened. The stage was decorated with cascading lights and a big star in the center. The brass band filled the stage in a semi-circle. The men dressed in their traditional red and green vests and black knickers with white socks, and the women wore long dresses. A small choir took the floor directly in front of the stage. The conductor stood on a small platform, lifted his baton, and the music began with "Joy to the World."

There was something about brass music that made Nicole feel awake and alive, in a way that even Papa's expensive sound system at home couldn't match. She could feel the brightness right inside her. She looked for Papa on stage, and saw him sitting next to Mr. Brunheim. It seemed Papa's eyes were shining as he played. She thought of Papa's music lessons. If Mr. Bernard had died in that prison camp, Papa may very well not be playing his golden trumpet tonight. The world seemed very strange sometimes.

Before intermission, the conductor turned to the audience and said, "Ladies and Gentlemen, I would like to announce that in our second half we will be presented with a rare and remarkable surprise. You are welcome to visit the refreshment tables in the vestibule, and if you wish to smoke, please do so outside."

As they reached the vestibule, Ashley grabbed Nicole's arm. "That's Stefan Brunheim over there," she whispered.

Nicole froze. She glanced across the vestibule and saw Stefan standing behind the soda table with two other teenage boys. She hadn't thought about the Brunheim boys coming to the concert, much less serving refreshments. She was extra thirsty right now, but no way would she go anywhere near him.

"Would you girls like some soda or cider?" Mama asked.

"No thanks," Nicole said. She turned so Stefan wouldn't be able to see her, and came nearly face to face with his brother, Andreas. He was holding hands with Marianna Platz, who was looking terribly bored as she fiddled with her hot pink cell phone. Nicole turned away from them as well.

"Mama, I think I'll have a soda," Ashley said.

From the corner of her eye Nicole followed them across the vestibule. Ashley stood back with her arms folded, looking at the floor as Mama bought two sodas and gave the money directly to Stefan Brunheim. "Are your other brothers here tonight?" she asked.

"Well — yes," Stefan said. "Except for Maximillian, he had to stay home with Mama. We came to watch Papa. It's kind of boring for me, so I volunteered to sell drinks."

"You're a true prince," Mama smiled.

Prince indeed — a prince of darkness, Nicole thought. She pictured herself marching up to the drink table, grabbing a bottle of soda and slamming it upside Stefan's pimpled forehead. How could he be so casual after trying to murder her and her sister?

She needed to use the bathroom, and absentmindedly walked into the men's room where she bumped into two boys dressed like sailors. For an instant she wondered why boys were in the women's room, but when she realized what she had done, she shrieked and backed out.

"That's okay," one of the sailor boys said. "People ask for autographs in the strangest of places."

She frowned. "An autograph? That's not quite what I'm here for."

The boys laughed and walked out into the vestibule, then went out a side door. Nicole hurried into the women's room, wondering what weird parents would let their kids dress up like that to go to a Christmas concert. Just what she needed, an autograph from the geek of the week. She chuckled, wishing she had been witty enough to say that to them. As she was washing her hands, she began to feel angry that she couldn't get a soda to quench her thirst, all because of that Brunheim delinquent standing behind the table. She filled her hand with cold water and sipped several handfuls until her hand was about frozen. Then she ran both hands under hot water as Ashley burst in and ran for a stall. "I have to go so bad," she said. "We better hurry, the lights are blinking."

"Don't forget to wash your hands," Nicole said. Out in the vestibule, she found her mother holding a bottle half filled with soda.

"There you are!" she said. "Do you want the rest of this before I throw it away?"

Nicole smiled, grateful to have her Mama over any other in the world. Even if she didn't know about the Brunheims, she knew her daughters. Nicole took the bottle and drank every drop. It was her favorite — cream soda. As she joined Ashley and her mother back at their seats, she smelled the distinct aroma of peppermint. She looked around to see where it may be coming from, but saw no clue.

The conductor stood on his platform and held out his hand. "Welcome back to our special concert," he said. "As I promised before intermission, we are about to be treated to a rare and remarkable surprise this evening. You may not realize that two of our band members have sons who sing in the Vienna Boys Choir. These boys have asked their director to permit the choir to come this evening for a visit. They have just finished a tour of Paris and Brussels, and have made a new Christmas album which is available for purchase after the concert."

The curtain opened to a group of about fifty boys dressed in sailor outfits. Nicole could see the two boys she bumped into in the men's room, standing in the back row. How could she have been so distracted that she couldn't tell those sailor outfits were choir uniforms? She wished she had been more gracious to them.

Presently the whole choir began without any orchestra, singing "Still, Still, Still." It was the most beautiful version of the carol she had ever heard. The Boys Choir sang seven more carols, then filed off the stage amid thunderous applause. The brass band

and community choir finished the concert with another carol that the whole audience joined in on, and again there was sustained applause as the lights gently brightened.

On the way to the car, Nicole made sure to avoid crossing paths with any of the Brunheim boys. After sitting for so long, her bruise had begun to throb with pain. The magic of the concert seemed to fade somewhat with the cold realization that she was a victim of something unresolved, and she had no idea how or when it might be resolved. If she told her parents now, there would be a big fuss about why she hadn't told them earlier. If she had told them earlier, there would be a big fuss all over town about how she got whacked on the butt with a golf ball, and the Brunheims would probably end up as enemies for life. If she tried to handle it herself, she was up against a whole family of boys who could be capable of all sorts of treachery. If she talked to teachers, then police would be called in and she would be marked as a tattletale. There seemed to be no way out. A thought came to her of Harold Bernard as a young boy being dragged off to a prison camp after the Gestapo murdered his mother. She wondered how he was ever able to enjoy his life or his music again after that.

As they were reaching the car, she could feel Papa's hand patting her on the back. He unlocked the doors and opened Mama's first, then hers.

"Tomorrow morning we'll go to Saint Martin

Church," Mama said. "Afterwards we'll get Kiachl at the Christmas Market."

"Oh, I've been dying for Kiachl!" Nicole said. "I want to get mine with lingonberry jam."

"Me too, me too!" said Ashley. "Mama, do you remember that time last year when we were in Zimt & Zucker, and that Englishman said he wanted to try a Key-ah-chill?"

Mama laughed. "Yes, I do. The baker was wagging his finger in the air. 'Here we say KEYuh-kul, or in Yiddish it's KICK-ul.' Then they had this big discussion about how you can have Catholic Kiachl with the sugar on the outer edge, and Protestant Kiachl with the sugar in the middle kneecap, and for little kids it's with Nutella."

"Tell me," Papa said. "Did the Englishman buy any?"

"He did," Mama said. "He bought a Protestant style. I don't know about the rest of you, but tomorrow I'm having mine with sauerkraut, the real traditional way."

❦ 6 ❧

Frost and Fire

UNDER THE COVERS in flannel pajamas, Nicole could not keep from shivering. She lifted the covers with both feet and let them drape beneath her legs like a sleeping bag. Strange thoughts crossed her mind, but she could not hold onto any one of them before another rattled along more disordered than the last. Her teeth began to chatter, and she thought of getting up to put another blanket on the bed, but felt too weak to even lift herself.

She knew there was something wrong, because no matter which way she turned she could not get comfortable. Her throat felt scratchy and hot, and her eyes heavy but sleepless. She could not, would not let herself come down with a cold or flu, no way! There would be church in the morning and Kiachl for breakfast, then off to the Old Town in Innsbruck for the Saint Nicholas and Krampus parade, the Christmas Market and the fairy tale performances at the Medieval Houses. And how could she miss the Golden Roof concert on the market square? She crossed her arms and held onto herself, and began to say prayers. "Dear angel of God, watch over my sleep," she whispered. "Dear Father in Heaven, fill me with love to do your will. Amen."

Some time during the night she drifted into a deep sleep, and didn't wake up until she felt Ashley sitting on her bed and touching her arm. "Hey Nicole?"

"Hmm? What?"

"It's going to be time for church. It's after eight already."

"Ashley?"

"What, Nicole? You're being weird. You never get up so late. Papa's already making coffee."

"Can you please tell Mama that I don't feel very well today? I think I'm getting a cold or something."

"Really? But you'll miss everything."

"I'm hoping not to. Maybe if I just sleep until Mama gets done with her real estate appointment."

"Okay, I'll go tell her." Ashley tiptoed out of the room and closed the door almost all the way.

Within a few minutes, Mama was in the room and

sitting on Nicole's bed, stroking through her hair with a cool hand. Papa stood in the doorway with a concerned frown. "You feel a little hot," Mama said. "I think you have a fever."

"I was shivering a lot last night. I think I just need to sleep some more. Maybe I'll be okay this afternoon."

Mama leaned over to kiss her forehead, and when she began to get up, she put a hand on Nicole's hip just barely above her bruise. The pressure caused her leg to seize in a cramp, but she forced herself not to react.

"Do you want me to stay back from church with you?"

"No, Mama. It's okay," she said. "I'm eleven, I'm not six."

"Well! Excuse me," she laughed. "Friedrich, honey — did you leave the empty pot on the coffee-maker? Something smells burned."

Papa sniffed the air. "I don't think so, there's still coffee in the pot. Maybe some spilled on the burner."

"Oh. I'll grab a cup before we go. Nicole sweetie, you sleep until we come back and we'll see how you feel. And don't worry, if we don't get to go to the Christmas Market today, there's always next weekend."

❦

SOMEHOW THE NIGHT of sleep took away the shivers, and Nicole felt already halfway better even if a little drained. She turned over her pillow and was about to settle her head when she thought she smelled burnt coffee. She got up on one elbow. A pungent smell irritated her nostrils, and she wondered if it might be just her imagination because of what her mother had said. It was probably wise to get up and make sure the coffeemaker was unplugged. It was supposed to be automatic shutoff, but Papa was overcautious and usually took the plug out, making the clock permanently wrong.

She padded barefoot into the kitchen and saw that the coffeemaker light was off, but it was still plugged in. She pulled out the plug, then made a detour to the bathroom before she found her way back to bed. The pillow was cool at first, but it warmed up quickly. Soon she was fast asleep.

She was in the middle of a dream when a shrill piercing sound jarred her awake. Her limbs were still numb as she became aware that the sound was the smoke alarm. It was not a dream, it was real — and the smell of smoke that she had smelled before was now much stronger. Her heart was slamming inside her chest. She lunged out of bed and grabbed some pants, pulling them on both legs at the same time and stuffing her bare feet into some high-top sneakers that poked from under her bed. She knew her father's absolute rule about fire in the house: GET OUT, GET OUT, GET OUT! Her head swam with thoughts of running into the kitchen to see if one of the phones was there, but she was also clear on Papa's words: "It takes only fifteen seconds for smoke to knock you down, don't even think of being a hero. GET OUT!"

She clambered out of her room and shut the door, groping through smoke toward the back door. She grabbed her ski coat, pulled open the door and got out on the porch to put the coat on. She reached back and pulled the door shut. Her ears were still whistling from the alarm.

She had to get the fire brigade right away, and to do that without a phone meant only one choice.

She had to go to the Brunheim Farm.

Her heart beat like a sledgehammer and for a second she felt like she would suffocate. How could she think those brutes were going to help? But the thought of her house burning down at Christmas time was a horror she would not entertain for a second. No time for crying now, just run! She began running as fast as she ever did, breathless and cramping, her legs spinning like in a cartoon, right for enemy territory. Snow crept into her sneakers and found its way into every crevice, partially melting into slush and chafing icy cold at her ankles.

By the time she reached the big farmhouse, she thought she was going to faint. Her head felt dizzy with fever. She ran for the front door and threw herself against it, banging with both fists. "Help! Help! My house is on fire!" she yelled, her throat parched.

The first Brunheim that reached the door was Blitzen. The dog scrambled around the side of the house through the snow and rushed right up to Nicole, rudely sniffing her body and nuzzling her to play. "Go away, Fang!" she yelled and pushed the dog away. She banged again on the door, and Mr. Brunheim pulled it open. Karl, the eldest son, was behind him. "Please help, please," she said. "Everybody's at church, and my house is on fire. The alarm —"

Mrs. Brunheim came running from the kitchen. She was a tall and sturdy woman, with red curly hair that made her look animated. "Oh my goodness, dear child. Step inside before you freeze to death. I'll call emergency."

There was a big clapper bell on a table in the hallway, and Mr. Brunheim picked it up and rang it. It was very loud, like a school bell. "Boys, grab the fire extinguishers and let's get over there!" he bellowed.

They may have been brutes, but they obeyed their father without blinking an eye. The three older boys got their shoes on and were out the door in less than a minute. They jumped into a pickup truck with two fire extinguishers, and were off. Mrs. Brunheim was on her phone, and Mr. Brunheim closed the big oak door and looked at Nicole.

"Your lips are blue, young lady. I think you need to stay here with Mrs. Brunheim till your parents come back."

"No!" she said much louder than she expected. "I mean, my Mama will be coming back from church any minute. She'll think I'm in the fire."

He shook his head and took Nicole by the hand. "All right. Come, we need to get there right away."

It had probably been about ten minutes from the time Nicole left the house until she got back with Mr. Brunheim. Already the boys had opened up the house and gone in, and were breaking open the hallway wall outside the girls' bedrooms. Nicole stood outside the open back door, watching with a mix of interest and horror. The fire was inside the wall, and had found its way up to the ceiling. Karl was breaking the wall with the claw of a hammer, and Stefan and Andreas were releasing the fire extinguishers on the smoldering wood. It took about twenty minutes to bury the floor in broken plaster, wood lathes and powdery foam from the fire extinguishers. The stink of burned wood filled the air.

"I think we have it all," Karl said, coming to the back door with the hammer hanging in his hand. He was tall, had the same dark hair as his kid brother Max, but also the mature look of a young man in college. "Looks like there was a bad wire in the wall."

Mr. Brunheim went into the house and opened several windows. A siren was wailing as the fire brigade came up the road and stopped in front. Four firemen jumped off the truck and rushed inside. "Is anybody in the house?" the fireman asked.

"Just us," called Karl. "The kid's out on the porch, the others are at church."

"What happened here? Smells like electrical fire," one of the firemen said.

"Yes, yes, we found a bad wire in the wall. I tripped it with the hammer to make sure the circuit was out," he said.

"Well, you are some brave lads," the fireman said. "We need to ask you to clear out and let us go through this place."

Mr. Brunheim came out of the house with a blanket in his hands. "Here, young lady. You're shivering something awful, let's get this around you. Are you sure you don't want to sit inside the warm car?"

She shook her head and backed up a step, arranging the blanket over her head so only her face was showing. She thought of telling Mr. Brunheim about what happened with the golf balls, but the boys were here — and if they knew she tattled, then she could be their target for the rest of her days. She was grateful that they came to put out the fire, but somehow their good deed did not erase the attack on her and Ashley. As it was, they probably didn't even know she got hit with their wild golfing.

There was a sudden commotion from the front of the house, and Nicole could hear car doors closing. She heard her mother's voice screaming in a tone she had never heard in her life. "Nicole! My Nicole! Oh my God, where is she?"

The next thing Nicole knew, Papa was on the back porch. He called out, "Julia! She's here, she's okay." He put both arms around Nicole and hugged her. "Are you all right?"

"I think so, Papa. I ran to get help from Mr. Brunheim."

"You ran over there?"

"The smoke alarm woke me up and I rushed out, like you always told me. What are we going to do about the house?"

"Well, we're going to do what anybody would do. Fix it."

Mama came running with Ashley right behind. She put both hands on Nicole's face and kissed her several times. "Oh, I'm so sorry, sweetheart. I thought I smelled something burning. We never should have left the house."

Ashley stood with her hands crossed at her neck. "Mama, it smells terrible." She pulled open Nicole's blanket and joined her inside it, wrapping it tightly around herself.

Mr. Brunheim said, "So sorry about this mess. She's a smart girl, she did all the right things."

"I don't know how we can ever thank you and the boys," Mama said. "You're such a good neighbor."

"If you need to stay out of the house, you let me know and we can prepare our extra room."

"Well, Mr. Brunheim — we sure have our hands

full," Mama said. "Thank you. We'll see what the fire inspector says and try to get this cleaned up."

"Glad we could help. I'd better get the boys back home. The cows are going to be kicking up a fuss if we don't get them milked pretty soon."

After the Brunheims left, Mama put her hands up to her eyes and began to cry.

ꕀ 7 ꕀ

A Light in Darkness

THE FIRE BRIGADE was gone. The inspector found that a wire had been frayed inside the wall, probably caused by a hungry mouse chewing through the insulation. He turned off the electricity to that circuit and declared the house safe. "I'll write up your damage report for insurance," he said. "Now we don't stand around and supervise, but you're required to throw away all food in your kitchen."

Inside the house, Mama didn't even wait to take her coat off. She crouched before Nicole, lifted her leg from behind the knee and pulled off one sneaker. "Before you take another breath, Nicole Kinders, you're going to get your bare feet out of these frozen things," she said, then did the same with her other leg. "Now just give me a minute and we'll go upstairs and get you a hot bath. I'm not going to have my brave daughter catching pneumonia."

"Thanks, Mama," she said, shivering and feeling no less miserable. All her life Nicole loved being in this corner of the village, living along the floor of the mountains in the old beam and stucco house that Mama and Papa had found right after they were married. For her it was a storybook home, with flower boxes on the windows and delicate designs painted around the window frames. But now the house seemed isolated, a tiny island in an endless landscape of winter. It was haunted with the acrid smell of smoke and the soggy wreckage strewn through the downstairs hallway, and didn't feel very much like home.

Papa was on his phone already, and Mama took hers out and called the American doctor to change her real estate appointment. While she talked, she went into the kitchen and opened a drawer, pulled out some towels, and brought the towels to Nicole. She motioned for her to put them on her feet, and Ashley took the bunch and helped unfold them. Mama finished the call and stood looking at the girls.

"Your feet have all black on them," Ashley said. "Oh my gosh! They're freezing cold."

"I think they're numb," Nicole said. "How am I going to get some new clothes to wear? We can't get to our rooms."

Mama said, "Don't worry about that. There are two

baskets of fresh laundry upstairs." Her phone rang again, this time with Grandma's ringtone. She looked at it and put it to her ear. "Mama?" She turned her back to the girls and walked to a corner of the front entry hall.

Papa meanwhile was on his phone with Marcel Bouchon, a handyman from town whom people called Frenchy. "I'm sorry to bother you on a weekend," he said. "We've had a fire and I need help right away."

Marcel Bouchon hailed from a family of plasterers, and he had many additional talents. He was short and strong, and had what Papa said was an abundance of personality. He had been married, but tragically lost his wife and son in a car wreck when the boy was seven years old. To ease his mind he built clocks and moving figurines as a hobby, delighting people with his window displays in many shops. Papa had hired him three years ago to remodel the upstairs bathroom, and was pleasantly surprised when Marcel took it upon himself to repair the heirloom clock that had been broken for years. Nicole was fascinated with his patient tinkering, and kept him company all through the clock repair project by helping hold the tiny tools. He became close to the girls since then, and at Christmas each year would give them gifts he created by hand. Last year he made them a small carousel with real working horses and miniature children riding. It had a Thorens movement from an old Swiss music box, and sometimes when Nicole felt lonesome or sad, she would start the carousel and listen to the music because it was sure to make her smile.

Nicole knew her mother was just finished talking with Grandma because she came back from the front hall with her face more relaxed and her voice lower. Grandma always seemed to know how to put things in order. Mama put the phone down and said, "Let's go, Nicole. Time for your beauty spa."

There was only a faint trace of smoke odor in the upstairs rooms, as that part of the house was well separated from the girls' bedrooms. Nicole stood on the warm bathroom carpet. She watched as her mother turned on the water and put her hand under the spout to test it, then took the container of body wash and squirt some under the spout. Sweet smelling bubbles filled the tub.

"How is she going to get the black off her feet?" Ashley asked.

"That will come off with soap," Mama said, wiping her hands on a towel. "Now you girls can stay here while Papa and I take care of business," she said, pulling a folded towel out of the linen closet. "There are clean clothes in the laundry baskets. Please try to keep things folded, and put your used clothes in the empty basket."

"Thank you, Mama." Nicole dipped her hand into the tub and swished the water around to make more bubbles. It was not as hot as she usually liked it. She reached over to turn the valve all the way hot.

"Do you still feel sick?" Ashley asked.

"My throat is really sore." She took off her clothes and eased into the tub.

"Are you hungry? I made Papa buy two extra Kiachln to take home for you. We left them in the car in the commotion."

"Thanks, Ashley. Maybe afterwards. I don't know if I have much appetite."

"I'm going to go get them out of the car so they won't get frozen. Do you need me to stay with you?"

"No, it's okay. I'm just going to soak a while."

"I can't believe you went to their house, Nicole. Did you see Max? Did they say anything?"

"No, he wasn't even there. I was petrified the whole time, worse than the fire. I don't even think they know they hit me. They're so lame, anyway. And I'm stuck looking like a red butt baboon from the Nature Channel."

"It's not quite that bad," Ashley said. "At least you don't have a tail."

"Shut u-up," she laughed as Ashley left the bathroom and closed the door.

The hot water felt magnificent. Nicole let herself sink all the way to her chin. She closed her eyes, thinking of everything that had happened over the weekend. Where was all the magic that was supposed to be revealed? So far it seemed that only bad things happened. She got hit with a golf ball, got a fever and had to miss church, had to escape a fire in her house, and right now was missing all the Saint Nicholas festivities in the Old Town.

With her eyes shut, she could see a nighttime sky of tiny dots floating in motion. She squeezed them a little tighter and the dots exploded into a fascinating universe of stars that continued swirling all by themselves. The stars spun out away from her at first, then spun back to converge into a circular shape that began to take the distinct form of an Aztec sun, just like Boznik's hand tattoo.

She jerked her eyes open, and the bathroom wobbled back into focus. Her heart was throbbing in the sides of her neck. Was that image supposed to be part of the magic? If it was, she didn't want any more of it. The next time she saw Boznik at his market stall, she was going to give him back the candy cane. He promised if she didn't like it, she would not have to pay. But how could she give him back this thing she had already opened and tasted?

She noticed her bath was beginning to cool. Slowly she sat forward and opened the drain, watching the water spin into a whirlpool. She took a deep breath and stood up, pulling the shower curtain closed. She ran the shower extra hot and gave herself a vigorous shampooing, then made sure the black dye from her sneakers was completely off her feet.

Her favorite jeans were with the folded clothes, one bit of good fortune. She finished dressing and drying her hair, then brushed with her mother's hairbrush.

As she opened the bathroom door, she could hear noises from downstairs. She pulled on some thick socks and unthinkingly started down the stairs two at a time as she usually took them, but stopped abruptly after the first foot landed. It felt like her leg was going to telescope up into her insides. She slowed down and took the rest of the stairs one at a time.

MARCEL BOUCHON HAD already come and set up shop in the hallway. All the pieces of broken lathe and plaster were gone from the floor, and he was kneeling on thick rubber kneepads. He had a white mask on that made him look like a doctor, and blue rubber gloves on his hands. He was using the biggest, loudest vacuum cleaner she had ever heard, with a hose like an elephant's trunk. Everybody stood watching as he sucked up every bit of the plaster crumbs and fire extinguisher waste from the floor and carpet. When he finished that, he rolled up the carpet and took it out the back door. Once again with the vacuum, he went over the whole hallway and then went into the broken parts of the wall and cleared them as well. Next he brought in a container of white vinegar and a big plastic bucket. Papa took the bucket into the kitchen and filled it halfway with water. Marcel opened the vinegar and poured some into the water.

In and out the back door he went, first getting

a ladder, then washing the ceiling and walls, then dumping out the black wash water in the snow and coming back for a refill. He went over the walls again, then got back on his kneepads to do the floor. Three complete washings, and the smoke smell was reduced and somewhat tamed by the odor of vinegar.

Finally he took off his mask and smiled. "That was the hard part," he announced. "I'll leave this vinegar for you to put in a few saucers around the house, it will help keep the smoky smell down. Whatever you do, don't be spraying any chemical air fresheners, they're poison and they only add, they don't subtract."

Again he went to his truck and brought back a big roll of clear plastic and some duct tape. From his pocket he took a knife, cut a big square from the plastic, and got up on his ladder to tape the plastic over the hole in the wall.

"Tomorrow we have to get the electrician in here and replace the wire and the plug outlet," he said. "Then we can fix the wall."

"Hey Frenchy?" Ashley said.

"Please call him Mr. Bouchon," Papa said.

"Mr. Bouchon, can we go in our rooms now?"

"I don't see why not. You might not want to sleep in them tonight. Just keep the windows open a little and put all the linens through the wash. For the clothes, you should take them to the cleaners and see if they come back without a smoky smell. If they still smell, you have to put them in the insurance pile."

"Well, I can't believe my eyes," Mama said. "In just two hours you made this place look almost normal."

"I'm so glad I could help," he said.

Papa helped Marcel carry his equipment back to his truck. It was midafternoon, still light outside. When Papa came back in, he went into the kitchen and took the sponge out of Mama's hand, tossed it into the sink, and put his arms around her. Nicole could see them kissing as Papa lifted Mama off the floor. "I told you we were going to have fun today," he said.

"If this is fun for you, then you better report to the mental hospital," she said.

"Well, I'll admit it's not really fun," Papa said. "But it could have been a lot worse."

"That doesn't make me feel any better," she said.

"Well, Julia, you should feel better. We still have our daughter and we still have our home. That is the very best gift I could ask for." He took the sponge from the sink and got some spray cleaner, and washed the kitchen table and chairs. He rinsed the sponge out and then washed the table again.

"You're right, Friedrich. But I feel like I just got punched in the stomach. Look at all that has to be done! Every cupboard has to be emptied and scrubbed, all the food has to be thrown away. Every surface has to be cleaned. The girls are going to be hungry and there will be nothing to eat."

"Mama?" Nicole said. "We still have the Kiachln. Ashley put them in the study. There's no smoke in there."

"Thank you, Nicole. Your voice sounds hoarse, how are you feeling?"

"I still feel achy and I have a bad sore throat."

"Come here and let me look. Okay, I think you need to stay home from school tomorrow. I'll be here for the workmen, and if you feel better you can come food shopping with me."

"I have an idea," Papa said. "Why don't I tackle the kitchen, and you can grab all the linens and get them through the wash. It's just the girls' bed and bathroom linens."

"Where are we going to sleep tonight?" Ashley asked.

"Well, Grandma said we should go over there," Mama said. "But I didn't think it was a good idea with Nicole being sick. There's plenty of room for two sleeping mats in the reading nook upstairs, and we can get the sleeping bags from the closet."

There was the sound of a car pulling up to the carport. Ashley raced for the front door and pulled it open so fast that the new wreath flapped and bounced against the door. "It's Grandpa and Grandma!" she said.

Grandpa came in first, carrying a large sack in each hand. He was tall and had silver hair and a trim beard, and a small bald spot on the back of his head. "The troops have arrived," he said. "What are you doing, running a cigar lounge in here?"

"Indeed!" Papa said. "Such a nice surprise to see you." Grandpa put the sacks on the table and reached into one of them, pulling out bottles of water. "Who needs some water?"

"I do," Nicole said.

"I think everybody needs it," Mama said.

Grandma came in the front door backwards, holding a box in front of her. "Hello, everybody!" she chimed. She looked exactly like Mama except for a few extra lines around her eyes and some gray edges to her hair. She was fifteen years younger than Grandpa, and he often called her his June bride. She swung the door closed with her hip, then brought the box to the table. "Some chicken for Sunday dinner tonight," she said in a tone she would use to tell a secret. "Baked in a pot with wine and potatoes and parsnips. It just needs twenty minutes in the oven. And not one, but two bottles of wine." She gave Mama a big hug and kisses, then peeled off her coat and said, "Okay, where do we begin?"

"I really wasn't expecting you to do all this," Mama said. "Why didn't you tell me you were coming?"

"Sometimes it's just better for me to do things and not talk," Grandma said.

"Ohhh — thank you so much. And such a nice

dinner," she said. "Friedrich is taking charge of the kitchen, and I need to put the linens in the wash."

"Well, let's you and I get that started right now," Grandma said. "Now wait till I tell you the latest news about your brother. Johan's coming from Zurich for Christmas, and he's bringing Pascale again. They'll stay with us till New Year's Day."

"Coming in his new Mercedes, no doubt?"

"Well, yes. But wait, there's more. This time there'll be an extra passenger."

Mama looked quizzically at Grandma, then her eyes lit up. "Nooo — really? At last I'm going to be an aunty?"

Ashley jumped up and down, then spun in a circle with her arms outstretched. "We're going to have a cousin! We're going to have a cousin!"

"And I'll turn into an uncle!" Papa said.

"That's my son," Grandpa said. "Now if only they'll get married." He hugged Nicole and then twisted open a bottle of water for her. "And here's our local hero," he said. "We're all very proud of you, Nicole. You're a Girl Guide of the highest order."

Ashley ran to the table and sat at her usual seat, one leg tucked underneath her. Grandpa kissed her on top of her head, then opened another bottle of water and put it in front of her. "You girls are quite the stars," he said. "Grandma and I saw you on the news with Saint Nicholas and Krampus."

"Really? We didn't see it," Nicole said. "Maybe we can find it on the Internet." She started drinking and found herself needing the entire bottle. "That was at the Christmas tree place yesterday. Our tree used to smell nice, but now everything smells like smoke and vinegar."

"Will we have to get a new Christmas tree?" Ashley asked.

"Probably," Grandpa said. "You don't want to have your nice decorations touching a smoky tree."

"It's a good thing we didn't decorate it yet," Nicole said. "We were supposed to put lights on yesterday, but we had Papa's Christmas concert."

"Lucky for that," Grandpa said. He took off his coat and hung it over a chair. "Friedrich, I don't want to get in your way. But if you need me to help, I'm here."

"I think I'm okay for now," Papa said. "How about taking that Christmas tree outside for the squirrels and birds?"

"Will do," Grandpa said. "Now you girls come with me."

❧ ✱ ☙

NICOLE AND ASHLEY followed Grandpa into the parlor and stood before the tree. Patterns of Jack Frost were forming on the front picture window as the sun began to set. Grandpa scratched his beard and then stroked over his chin. "You know, this is the first time I've ever taken down a Christmas tree before Christmas, and I'm almost a hundred years old."

"You are no-ot," Ashley said.

"Mama said you're eighty-three," Nicole said.

"Guess I can't fool you two. Did I ever tell you about the Ardennes Forest Christmas tree?"

"Not yet," Ashley said. "Tell us."

"Well, this happened a long, long time ago. It was in World War Two, December 1944. The German army was pushing through the Ardennes Forest on their way to Antwerp. By this time, Germany was grabbing anybody they could and putting them in uniform, including me. I was fifteen years old."

"Really? That's terrible," Nicole said.

"We came upon this American in the middle of nowhere, and we captured him as a prisoner of war. Things were pretty bad, and most of the time prisoners were shot. But one of our guys could understand a little English, and this American told us how his plane got shot down. He had no parachute. He dropped like a rock and happened to land in a huge pine tree. He said he bounced from branch to branch all the way to the bottom till he was on the ground with only a few cuts and scratches. At first we didn't believe him, but when he brought us to the tree we could see that something crashed down one whole side of it. Well, nobody was going to shoot him after all that, so we had a big party for the American."

"That is excellent," Nicole said. "What happened then?"

"Well, it was getting to be Christmas time. The American couldn't speak German, but he knew Tannenbaum meant Christmas tree. These guys went out in the forest to cut one, and the American found a pine tree instead of a fir tree. He was all excited about it, but we told him it was a Kieferbaum, not a Tannenbaum. Everybody had a few laughs, and he learned a lesson about the proper Christmas tree."

"Did they all have Christmas together?" Nicole asked.

"Well, there wasn't much heavenly peace in the battle zone," he said. "But I guess we did okay. We put the tree in a deserted barn and made our camp there. The farmhouse was bombed out, but we found some food in the ruins. Every meal we had, we thought it might be our last. We gave the American some food, and he gave us some chocolate bars he had in his jacket. But later I saw him sitting on a rock, heaping fresh snow into his canteen cup. He took out a little envelope and mixed some lemonade powder into the snow. He was making dessert for himself right in the middle of a war."

Ashley laughed and said, "He was eating yellow snow!"

Grandpa lifted Ashley in his arms and rubbed his nose against hers. "Are you being a little Katzenjammer Kid?"

"Let Grandpa tell his story," Nicole said.

"Now," Grandpa said as he brought Ashley back to her feet, "there was a priest that happened to be driving along the forest road, and he saw our encampment so he stopped. He said he was going to have Mass. It wasn't Christmas Day yet, but it might be the only time he could have Mass while we were all still alive. Everybody watched him set up an altar on the front of his jeep. While he said Mass the snow started to fall. It got to be a big snowstorm, and that was the last we saw of the American."

"He got away?" Nicole asked.

"Well, a firefight broke out that day, and some say he got shot. But when we searched through the snow we never found him, only some spots of blood. We were pretty sure he found his way back to his own troops."

"So maybe he has grandchildren in America now," Nicole said. Her mind swam with thoughts of Grandpa being stuck at war in the forest. She could not imagine her fifteen-year-old neighbor Stefan Brunheim being a soldier, and wondered what Grandpa must have been like at that age.

"So you see," he said. "Even in a war people find a Christmas tree."

"There were two Christmas trees," Ashley said.

"You're so right!" he said. "And if it wasn't for each of those trees, then that Christmas would have been a whole lot different."

"How come people get a Christmas tree?" Nicole asked. "How did it all start?"

"Oh, that started back in the earliest times," he said. "The Druids and the ancient Romans had celebrations around the winter solstice. It was the darkest day of the year, and they would light bonfires to bring light into the darkness, and they would decorate their houses with holly or greens because they wanted to have something green and alive in the dead of winter. When Christianity began, people still wanted their old traditions. So the Christians adopted the Christmas tree as a symbol of life in winter. We light candles, we hang lights on our trees and our houses. Most religions have traditions to bring light into the darkness. You don't have to be Christian to celebrate those things."

She watched Grandpa loosen the bolts in the Christmas tree stand. "Now you two help hold up the tree for me so it won't keel over, okay?"

"So Christmas started even before Baby Jesus?" Nicole asked.

"Not Christmas, but winter festivals," Grandpa said. "Nobody knows for sure exactly what month Jesus was born. But since Jesus was a living light in all the world's darkness, then what better time to celebrate his birth than around the solstice?"

With a strong pull, he got the tree up out of the stand and carried it to the front door trailing needles behind him. Ashley hurried to the door to hold it open. "Can you put it where we can see it from the kitchen?"

"I'll do my best. Close the door after me. And when I come back in we'll clean up the pine needles and get that dinner in the oven.

Advent Calendar

EVERYTHING WAS SILENT upstairs except for the occasional ticking of snowflakes against the windows, and the faint background sound of her father's snoring. Nicole was wide awake. Tucked into her sleeping bag in the reading nook, she stared at the carved oaken beams around the ceiling. Over and over in her mind she thought about tonight, and became worried that she was singlehandedly ruining Christmas for the whole family. At dinnertime, her fever had risen while she was trying to enjoy Grandma's roasted chicken, and she felt miserable. Mama noticed that her face was red and her eyes were glassy, and made her lie down in the parlor.

Grandpa and Grandma had come into the parlor

to say goodbye, and when Grandpa offered to carry her upstairs to bed, she said, "Not this time, I don't want you to catch my germs."

Grandpa said that he wasn't worried, she had never made him sick before. But Nicole knew if anybody carried her, then her bruise would be right in the way and she would be in agony. When Grandpa leaned down to say goodbye, she shoved him away and screamed, "Why can't everybody just leave me alone? I said I can take my own self to bed!"

She could see the crestfallen look in his face as he stood back and shrank to a smaller size right before her eyes. "I was just going to kiss you good night," he said. Grandma held his hand and said, "Nicole's getting all grown up now, dearie. Let's go home, it's been a long day."

And then they were gone. She felt as if she had changed something permanently by her outburst. She was not getting so all grown up, even though she could see that was the message Grandpa got. She didn't know if she could ever take that back.

This was supposed to be a magical Christmas, and she was trying to make it a magical Christmas. Not only were things going wrong, but they were getting worse. And involving more people. It was time to do something about it.

It all came down to Boznik.

Or maybe it didn't. But she was blaming him anyway.

On the other hand, there was Max Brunheim. What in the world was up with him? Since his standoff with Isabelle Schubert, and then the escapade with the golf balls, he completely disappeared. Something was said about one of the boys having an accident, but that could have been any one of them. And nobody said anything about Max all during the time the Brunheims were putting out the fire.

Her stomach began to ache, and she realized she was not going to sleep any time soon. Her throat was dry and still very sore. She needed a glass of water. If she used the upstairs bathroom, she might wake up her parents, so she decided to go downstairs. When she got to the bottom of the stairs, she noticed that a strange light from outside the house was illuminating the kitchen and dining room. She could see upside-down pots and pans covering the counters, and plates piled everywhere there was space. The cupboard doors were all open, and the cupboards empty. She went into the bathroom and saw that the holly design towels were back in place. She ran the cold water and filled a cup, then sipped slowly so her throat would not burn. There was a bad taste at the back of her mouth that would not go away when she drank.

She passed by her bedroom door and followed the strange light to the kitchen windows, and what she saw outside caused her to gasp. On her left was a swirling gust of falling snow that drifted like a white ghost as it whooshed down from the Gartendorf peaks through the back fields. On her right was a perfectly clear sky lit by an almost full moon, glowing on the wave of snow and on the smoked Christmas tree that Grandpa had stuck into the snowbank. She knew that this window was the only place on Earth to witness this spectacle, and she was the only spectator. She watched the wave of snow shift here and there, now blowing snow all through the Christmas tree, then easing back and letting the moon shine again. Soon the moon was obscured and snow was swirling everywhere.

Nicole tiptoed back to her bedroom door and opened it a crack. It was very cold in her room, and she could see that some snow had sneaked through the window openings to dust the sills. It smelled of winter air. There in the vague snow light she could see her school sack with the candy cane still poking out. She shivered from her shoulders all the way to her feet. The thought came to her that if she wanted magic, and this thing was supposed to be magic, then she should just grab a hold of it, come what may. She reached for the candy cane and touched it. She slowly lifted it out of the school sack and peeled back the wrapper. She knew the inspector said all food was supposed to be thrown away, but this was wrapped and mostly away from the smoke. She put the end into her mouth.

No burst of peppermint.

There was a vague sweetness and some hint of spiced mint, yes — but the bad taste in her throat was not going away, nor was there even a hint of change in the room or in Nicole. She pulled the candy cane out of her mouth with a lip-popping sound, and waved it in the air as Boznik had done, like a wand. "The magic will be revealed," she said.

No sign of magic.

What should she expect? Was she about to fly around the room, or become invisible, or be instantly cured of her fever? What would she do with magical powers if she suddenly got some? Could she go back in time and make the fire not happen? Or ski with Ashley in a different direction instead of the Brunheim Farm?

Oh well, can't believe everything adults tell you. Mama always said watch out for people who are trying to sell you something. You'll get all sorts of promises, but what promises ever live up to your dreams? On the other hand, Boznik wasn't really trying to sell this, otherwise wouldn't he have been in a hurry to take her money? It was all too confusing to her.

She put the candy cane back inside her school sack, this time tucking it in the zippered pocket. See if it would climb out by itself now! She hurried out of the cold room into the warmth of the house, closing the door behind her. The moonlight was back again, lending a soft glow to the kitchen and dining room. A thought crept into her mind that maybe —

just maybe — there was indeed some magic tonight. All the while she was wondering about magic that was not happening, there before her very eyes was the spectacle of the moonlit snowfall. Maybe — just maybe — she didn't need to eat it, or hold it, or wave it like a wand.

But still, she intended to take the candy cane back to Boznik, the very first chance she had.

WHEN SHE WOKE up again it was morning, and sunlight was streaming in the arched window of the reading nook. Ashley was not on her sleeping mat, and her sleeping bag was arranged neatly with the pillow perfectly placed at the top. Nicole became aware of her mother's voice speaking English on the phone from the bedroom. An aroma of her dressed-up-for-business perfume wafted on the air. Nicole looked at the heirloom clock. It was almost nine-thirty. She could not remember ever sleeping so late.

Her throat was still sore, but was beginning to feel better. She stretched her arms as far as they possibly could go, wiggled her fingers, then wiped her eyes with her knuckles. Her hair was all over the place, and she fingered it back from her forehead to her pillow. She noticed that it was feeling thicker and fuller these days.

There were noises drifting upstairs from below.

Machine noises, and now banging. She remembered that the workmen were to be here today to work on the fire damage. Since the fire she had become curious about all that stuff inside the walls that she never thought about before. Seeing the beams and lathes made her want to find out. She sat up, feeling the lingering pain of her golf ball injury. Was this thing ever going to go away?

She stood up and walked into her mother's bedroom. Mama turned and smiled, still on her phone, and came to put her arm around Nicole. "Just a minute, sweetie," she barely whispered.

Nicole pointed to the bathroom door and then went in, surrounded with the mingled smells of her mother's beauty items. She washed her hands and face, then looked into the mirror. Her eyes seemed turquoise today, and her hair was very glossy. She raised her right eyebrow the way Max Brunheim would do at school when he was trying to make her laugh. It annoyed her that he was the one who inspired her to learn the trick. But it was fun anyway. She tried it with the left eyebrow, and then with both, and found herself laughing out loud at herself.

Mama was touching up the edges of her lipstick in the bedroom mirror when Nicole came back. "What's got you laughing?" she said.

"I just thought of something funny. Hey Mama? I think I'm feeling a little better today."

"Well, you slept like the dead," she said. "Ashley was humming and dancing all around, and Papa was winding the clock, and you didn't even stir."

"How come you're dressed all fancy?"

"If you want to find out, get some clothes on in a hurry and come with me. I was just about to call Aunt Valeria to come stay with you."

"Can she come, Mama? I wanted to watch Mr. Bouchon fix the wall downstairs."

"Well, Aunt Valeria just broke up with that Basil fellow she met on-line, and she needs to do some shopping therapy today. You know she gets very few personal days."

"Oh."

"Come over here."

"What?"

She put her hands on Nicole's shoulders and looked her in the eyes. "Did I tell you how very proud Papa and I are of you? That was a very brave thing you did, and I know how sick you felt."

Nicole nodded. "I don't like to think about it. Everything hurt and my throat killed, and I was feeling really grouchy."

"I think everybody had reason to be grouchy yesterday. But it's a new day, and tomorrow is the Feast of Saint Nicholas. Come now, get some clothes on and you can watch Mr. Bouchon work when we come home."

THEY DROVE OVER the bridge and past Boznik's market stall on their way to the rainbow colored houses at the Inn River. The snow that had fallen during the night merely dusted Innsbruck, even though it had left six centimeters on the eastern half of Gartendorf. Driving was not bad, and the day was mild. Their first stop was at the property her mother was showing Dr. Johnson.

While her mother was in the building, Nicole checked out the shopping list app on the phone. For fun she added Almdudler, to see what her mother's reaction would be to find a sugary soft drink on her shopping list. If she tried that on her father's phone, it would go unnoticed because he never used his phone for shopping, only for checking bar codes to compare prices. He preferred the apps that showed where the ski slopes and public toilets were, and what the weather was going to be wherever he had business. To get a bottle of Almdudler with him, all she needed to do was put it in the shopping cart — no electronics required.

By the time her mother came back to the car Nicole had played SpongeBob Tickle till her eyes goggled, then found herself scrolling through photos and changing everybody into Lego pictures. "Hey Mama, look — you and Papa as Legos!"

"Wow," she said. "Imagine how many Legos you'd need to actually make that? Now don't forget to change my pictures back to normal."

"I'm doing it each time, don't worry."

Mama started the car and turned the heat up. "Guess what? Dr. Johnson likes the place. He really likes it. I thought a chalet might be nicer, but he's more the city type, and it will be perfect for him. Three bedrooms, two bathrooms, and a gas fireplace!"

"So did he buy it?"

"He gave a deposit check and signed an agreement. So I'd say he's going to be an Innsbruck vacationer this winter."

"You're going to make a lot of money, aren't you?"

"Well, let's see how much we have left of it after we pay for the smoke damages."

"Papa said the insurance would pay."

"Well, they only pay so much, but it's good to be optimistic. Now what do you say, shall we go shopping?"

They ended up going through three different markets to replace most of the lost food. In the last shop, Nicole helped collect the spices from the shelf as Mama read the list from her phone. Then into the cart went mustard, mayonnaise, relish, pickles, jars of every comestible needed to restock the cupboards. When they got to the juice and drink aisle, Mama read off, "Almdudler? Hmm, Papa must want some for Saint Nicholas Eve. Let's get two bottles."

"Really?"

"Let's hurry now, we have a lot to do before Ashley comes home from school."

Back home, it took four trips to the car to bring in all the goods. Amid the hubbub of construction in the hallway, delivery of the girls' clothes from the cleaners (the stuffed animals would need extra time), a visit from the insurance adjuster, and a cleaning crew going over the parlor and the bedrooms, it seemed more like an airport than a kitchen. Nicole unpacked sacks and her mother organized the items left, right and in the refrigerator, and finally everything was packed away. Nicole wandered into the back hallway to watch Marcel Bouchon and his helper. There was a big white drop cloth all along the floor and a smell of paint. She could see that the burned parts of the wood inside the wall were now painted white.

"Hi, Mr. Bouchon," she said.

"Hello, Nicole!" he said, adjusting his tool belt. "Today the electrician put in the new wire and plug outlet, then we put the anti-smoke paint on the wood. Now we're going to close up the big hole."

"Can we sleep in our rooms tonight?"

"I know, I know — it's Saint Nicholas Eve," he said. "But I think you'd better stay upstairs till all this work is done."

"Oh." She watched the men use their noisy screw guns to fasten gypsum board they had cut to fit the hole. Next they mixed plaster and smoothed it on until the surface was perfect.

"Do you smell smoke now?" he asked.

"Not very much. Just a tiny bit."

"By the time we get done, the smell should be mostly gone," he said.

Mama came over carrying a tray with four glasses of water. "Marcel and Kasimir, thanks so much for all your work. Here, have some water. Nicole, you need to keep drinking and flush that flu bug out of you."

"Thanks, Mama."

There was a sound of the front door closing hard, and Ashley glided in dance steps across the kitchen while pulling off her school sack, hat and coat all at once. "Wait till I tell you, wait till I tell you!" she announced.

"What?"

"Max Brunheim has eight stitches right through his left eyebrow!"

Nicole froze, giving a look of dire warning to Ashley as she came closer. "Oh — really?"

"Hello, sweetheart," Mama said, ruffling Ashley's hair. "That sounds terribly painful, poor Max. Is his vision all right?"

"He can see okay, but he has a rude looking black eye."

"Oh, dear. Well, how was your day?"

"It was excellent, Mama. I had time before the

tram, so I ran up to Boznik and bought a Saint Nicholas cookie. I wanted to get more but I didn't take enough money."

"Mama bought Almdudler for tonight," Nicole said.

Marcel and his helper finished their water, and handed the glasses back to Mama. She took the extra water glass and gave it to Ashley. "Here you go."

Ashley took the glass and drank so fast that water spilled down both sides of her chin.

"Now that you girls are both here," Marcel said, sending a quick wink to Mama, "I need to ask your opinion on something."

"What do you want to know?" Ashley chimed, nudging Nicole with her elbow.

Nicole nudged her right back. "Shush," she hissed under her breath.

"Once we get finished painting here, I have something that I would like you girls to have that you can hang on the wall. I brought it in my truck today, and if you like it, then you can keep it forever."

"What is it?" they both asked at once.

"Kasimir, can you go out to the truck and carry that box in here, please?" he said. His helper nodded and trundled out the back door. In a minute he came back with a large carton box. Marcel placed the carton box on the drop cloth and slowly opened the four flaps. Inside was a display case of polished mahogany and glass. It had twenty-five compartments, each with its own glass door, and each door with its own doorknob.

"That is beautiful!" Nicole said.

"Ah, but that's not all," he said. He lifted out the display case, and beneath it was an assortment of what appeared to be Christmas tree ornaments, each one different and separated by cardboard sections. "This is an animated Advent calendar. I started it a long time ago for little Roger — but it's been in the box all this time."

"I'm sorry that accident happened," Nicole said.

"Mama said Roger would be twelve," Ashley said. "Does it make you sad sometimes?"

"Ah, yes," he sighed. "But I think Roger would want you to have this." He picked up the first piece and held it in his hand. It fit his palm, and stood as tall as his fingers. He pressed a small button and the scene lit up inside. It was a fireplace hearth with a realis-tic looking fire, and tiny shoes lined up at its edge. A miniature cat began to chase a mouse in circles while a soft chiming music box played "Brahms Lullaby."

Both girls stood transfixed. Nicole reached out for the piece, and Mr. Bouchon placed it into her hands. The fireplace mantel was carved with a lion's head in the center, and had claw feet. The miniature cat and mouse had realistic fur and tiny glowing eyes. Above the hearth was a dainty portrait of a woman with a little boy standing at her knee.

"Now each of the scenes has a number from one

to twenty-five," he said. "After the wall is painted, we can hang the display case and put all the scenes in the compartments. Then each day of December you take out one scene as you get closer and closer to Christmas."

"How did you make all these?" Nicole asked. "They're so perfectly detailed. Did you see these, Mama?"

"Yes, yes — I see. This is quite an impressive present. I'm a little overwhelmed," she said.

"I understand, Mrs. Kinders. But it would be a shame for them to collect dust in the back of my shop. And how could I sell them to a stranger? They're all made from old watches and clocks. Some parts come from cuckoo clocks, so you'll find little birdies flying about. Each one has a movement from an old music box. There's one of Saint Nicholas dropping gold into the window of the poor maidens so they could have a dowry — that one is for December 6. My favorite is the Nativity. That one has Mary holding the baby and rocking back and forth while Joseph watches, and three angels with trumpets flying in a circle over the stable."

"Can we see it?" Ashley said.

The doorbell rang.

"Excuse me a second," Mama said. "I'll be right back."

Nicole and Ashley darted a look at each other,

and Ashley shrugged. "Maybe it's package delivery," she said, then whispered, "Wait till I tell you."

"Hush yourself," Nicole whispered.

Mama came back with Aunt Valeria, her younger sister who looked very much like her except for a tousled mane of deep auburn hair and dark eyes. She was a bit on the fresh side, as Papa would say. She believed a woman should always look as if she just stepped out of a convertible. Nicole had heard her say that many times. Aunt Valeria was the maid of honor at Mama's wedding thirteen years ago, and had caught the bouquet. Nobody, least of all the young men who were in love with Valeria, could understand why she never married. But when she waltzed into the hallway now with her shopping bag of plenty, she looked at Marcel Bouchon and Marcel Bouchon looked at her, and Nicole wondered if they might be long lost friends.

Mama said, "Valeria, this is Marcel Bouchon, our dear house doctor and his assistant Kasimir. They've done a miraculous job of fixing our fire damage."

"A pleasure," Aunt Valeria said as she tugged off her long leather glove and held out her hand to Marcel. Her eyes fluttered and she blushed a little when he took her hand.

"Please excuse my rough hands," he said.

"Hi, Aunt Valeria!" Ashley said. "You should see what Mr. Bouchon made."

"Hi, Aunty," Nicole said, holding up the fireplace scene for her to see. "Mama almost got you to babysit for me today."

"I'd be glad to come stay with you anytime, doll face. My two favorite nieces in all of Austria!"

"We're your only nieces," Nicole said.

"That makes you all the more special," she said. "Why, that's an enchanting creation. Look at that little tiny mousie! He even has whiskers! Marcel, did you really make this?"

"I did," he said.

"Speaking of staying," Mama said, "it is the Eve of Saint Nicholas, and we're having a wonderful dinner. Please plan on celebrating with us. I would like to ask Mr. Bouchon and Kasimir to join us as well. Gentlemen, would you please?"

Marcel and Kasimir eyed each other, then nodded. "Yes, thank you," Marcel said. "That would be lovely. We'll clean up now and go home to change out of our work clothes."

"I will bring magic tricks," Kasimir smiled with his crooked teeth.

"Wonderful. Friedrich will be bringing home Saint Nicholas cookies and chocolate, and the girls will be putting out their best polished shoes. And tonight we will all be putting more pieces of straw in the manger for our good deeds. Heaven knows everybody did their part."

"I have brand new red high heels to put out," Aunt Valeria said with a naughty smile.

"We don't need any lightning strikes here, darling," Mama said. "Why don't you wear the shoes for our company?"

❦

UPSTAIRS AS NICOLE was brushing her hair for dinner, Ashley slipped into the bathroom and closed the door. "You should have seen it, Nicole."

"What happened to Max?" she said.

"He said he got hit in the eyebrow with a golf club. His brother Stefan was swinging it, and he got a concussion."

Nicole stopped brushing and reeled away from the mirror. It was beginning to feel like black magic. Hadn't she originally thought that Max might be hit by a golf swing? She stared at Ashley. "Was it on purpose?"

"Didn't say. I just heard Max and Andreas talking about how they were golfing from their field right in the snow, trying to scare away a couple of tourist skiers down on the trails.

"Tourists? Do I look like a tourist?" Nicole said, wagging the hairbrush.

"Well, wait till I tell you! I moved to a seat near Max and asked him if he was sure they were tourists, and he didn't say anything. So I told him it was us," she said, pointing a finger at herself. "I said he hit you in the stomach with a golf ball, and that you had internal bleeding."

"Ashley, you did not!"

"Did too. His face turned all white. I said that we had the fire in our house and you ran all the way over there to get help, but after everybody left, you collapsed and were spitting up blood."

Nicole put the hairbrush down and covered her mouth with both hands. "Ashley! You didn't. You didn't tell him that."

"Honestly, I did. I was really mad at him, and I told him that you were probably going to be in the hospital for a long time. I said, 'If my sister dies, you better not even think of showing up with flowers, because you won't be allowed.' Then he and his brother just deflated and went home like a couple of beaten dogs."

"Oh my gosh, Ashley. I don't think you did the right thing. What if they go home and tell their father and mother? Then Mr. Brunheim will come over here and see I'm not in the hospital, and he'll go home and tell the boys it was just a fake story. And Mama and Papa will know everything, which means I'll get my own personal taste of hell."

"They'll never tell their parents," Ashley said. "Don't you remember when Mr. Brunheim said if Stefan had to go to juvenile detention for stealing those iPods, then too bad, he would just have to take his punishment?"

"Yeah, and so what?"

"So why would they want to tell Mr. Brunheim, if he would let them go to juvenile detention?"

"But Ashley, I have to go to school anyway. They're going to see me with their own two eyes."

"Or in Max's case, eye and a half," Ashley said. "So big deal, let them suffer for a day. They can have Krampus night tonight, for all I care."

Nicole took a deep breath that caught halfway in and choked her into a coughing fit. When she recovered she wheezed, "Ashley, you're a terror sometimes. You better hope this doesn't turn into something that gets us both in trouble."

❦ 9 ❧

The Feast of Saint Nicholas

DINNER ON SAINT NICHOLAS EVE was delightful in every possible way except for the gnawing fear in the pit of Nicole's stomach that there would be a knock on the door from Mr. Brunheim. Ashley was suffering no such fears, and was enjoying the feast with reckless abandon. Aunt Valeria and Marcel Bouchon were making eyes across the table at one another much of the time. Kasimir told stories of what Christmas was like in his native Warsaw, and performed some magic tricks. Papa poured out glasses of wine and later, cordials for the ladies and fine brandy for the men. Toward the end of the evening, Marcel went to the box of his Advent calendar creations and took out the piece for December 6. He put it on the table and touched a small button on the base, and immediately it lit up and began to move. The Saint Nicholas figure stood outside of an open window, and on the inside were three beautiful young ladies sleeping in a doll house bed with carved posts and an embroidered quilt. Saint Nicholas waved his arm and three nuggets of gold in his hand jingled on the windowsill as a music box movement chimed with "Beautiful Dreamer." When the music ended, the light turned off and the piece became still. Everybody stared at it for a moment longer, then began clapping.

"Viva Saint Nicholas!" said Kasimir as he raised his brandy glass.

"May he live in us all," said Papa with his glass in the air. "And may we always remember that God's gifts are meant to be shared."

Mama said, "Thank you all for coming and making this a special feast. Now let's put our straw in the manger for our good deeds, from the youngest up."

Nicole watched as Ashley counted out her pieces of straw from the small bundle and placed them into the birch manger. When it became her turn, Nicole couldn't bring herself to put in any straw. She knew she helped her mother with shopping and arranging the kitchen, and did her school work faithfully, not to speak of remembering to take her hair out of the drain after showering, and her plates to the sink after meals. But Nicole passed the bundle on to Aunt Valeria. "I don't think I'm ready to put mine in just yet," she said.

Nobody said a word about it. Each person counted out pieces of straw according to his own good deeds, and placed them into the manger. Papa finished with his, then brought out his trumpet. He played "O Come, O Come, Emmanuel," and on the second verse he was joined by Marcel's voice in French, Kasimir's voice in Polish, and the rest of the family's voices in German.

BEFORE SHE WENT to bed, Nicole begged her mother to let her stay home from school just one more day. "My throat is still sore, and I really want to watch Mr. Bouchon finish the work. I want to help him put the Advent calendar on the wall."

"There'll be plenty of time for that after school," she said. "You've missed lessons already, and you really shouldn't fall behind. Besides, there will be nobody home and Aunt Valeria will be at work."

What she told her mother was only partly true. She did want to watch Marcel, but she really needed to stay home another day because she wasn't about to let the Brunheim boys see her alive and well just yet. That would be letting them off way too easy. She was starting to like that Ashley had told them that dreadful story about her spitting up blood. She felt she was no longer under their power, but that they were now under hers. To give that up by merely walking into school, and then actually sitting next to Max Brunheim in class, was unthinkable. Plus, she needed time to think about what she would say to Max.

And just as important, or maybe even more important, she needed to take the candy cane back to Boznik.

She thought of making herself vomit, but that would be risky because with her stomach, she could end up sick all day. Then she thought it might be best to miss the school tram and get on a later city tram. That way nobody would see her except for Ashley, who wasn't likely to stop her. It was supposed to be cold and snowy, so she would have to bundle up if she expected to skip school. The school had already been notified that she was sick Monday, so no inquiry would be made if she continued to be absent. Her empty seat would be a glaring reminder to Max all through classes that every minute her seat was empty was one minute closer to his reckoning.

She got up early and went downstairs, suddenly remembering it was Saint Nicholas Day. The shoes that she and Ashley put out last night were full of goodies. She was almost ready to run back upstairs to wake Ashley up, but decided their surprises could wait just a while longer until everybody came down.

She went into her room to get dressed. Long

underwear, thermal socks, layers on top as if she were dressing for a ski day at Patscherkofel resort. She went into the bathroom and washed her face with cool water, as the clothing was making her feel a little too warm. She brushed her hair back into a ponytail. In her room again, she rummaged around in her sock drawer and found two hand warmer packets. She tucked them into the zippered pocket of her school sack next to the candy cane. She looked into the drawer again, grabbed an extra pair of thermal socks and put them in as well. She was ready for the outdoors.

Papa was preparing coffee in the kitchen by now, dressed in a business suit and thumbing over his telephone screen. "Good morning, Nicole," he said, leaning forward to kiss her on the forehead. "Did you see your goodies?"

"Oh, I sure did. I wanted to wait —"

Before Nicole could finish, Ashley came barreling down from the reading nook two stairs at a time. She somehow flubbed the last step, which sent her sprawling awkwardly across the kitchen directly into Nicole. "Ashley, you sound like an elephant!" she said, doing her best to keep Ashley from hitting the floor. "You better not try that for a dance routine."

"Good thing you caught me. I was just about to crash and burn," she said, laughing at herself. "I was in a hurry to see my goodies."

"You think?" Nicole said. "It looked like you were in a hurry to bash your head open."

Ashley laughed so hard that her effort to cover her face turned into a feeble wave of limp fingers across her nose before she doubled over in uncontrolled belly laughs. Nicole caught the laughter and joined in for the best laugh she'd had in a long time. She caught her breath and stood straight, noticing the broad smile on her father's face as he stood watching them.

"Hyenas. I have two laughing hyenas for children," he said. He wrapped an arm around each of them and hugged them to his face.

"What about Mama?" Nicole asked.

"I'm right here," Mama said from the top of the stairs in her plaid footie pajamas. "I thought I heard an avalanche and figured I better come out and join the fun. How nice to begin this day with the sound of my girls laughing."

"Happy Saint Nicholas Day," both girls said.

"Come now, let's go see your goodies," Papa said.

"Yes, let's!" Mama said. "Thanks for letting me get that extra bit of sleep. The workmen won't be here till nine, and I'll have time to get myself ready for work."

"Is Mr. Bouchon going to be here all day?" Nicole asked.

"I imagine he is. There's still a bit of work to be done, so I'm sure you'll see him when you come home from school."

"Oh," she said, half wishing she could count on Marcel to be finished early so she could slip home undetected. She wasn't sure how she was going to spend the school day yet. She followed Ashley and her parents into the parlor, then took her shoe full of goodies to the sofa. An orange dropped into her lap as she tipped the shoe, and then came chocolate Saint Nicholas figures wrapped in foil, a beautiful sparkle pen, packets of SpongeBob and Barbapapa stickers, fingernail design stickers, lip gloss and two shades of nail polish. At last there was a ten euro note folded into a tiny origami square. "This is so cool!" she said. "Every single thing I got is perfect. And more money I can save to get my phone."

Ashley had similar gifts poured out on the floor where she sat. "I want to put some of my nail polish on now," she said.

"You probably only have time to do two fingers," Papa said. "Maybe it's best to wait till you come home."

"Ohhh. Okay, then. I should go get ready for school."

"Sweetie, make sure you dress warm," Mama said. "It's expected to be very cold today." She kissed Ashley and then came to give Nicole a big hug and kiss. "You girls are my best gift ever."

"I love you, Mama," Nicole said.

After her mother went back upstairs, Nicole collected her gifts and carried them to her room. She put the chocolates into her school sack and everything else on top of her dresser. She gathered her school sack, plus her best thermal lined knit hat and ski gloves, and placed them in the front entrance by the door with her warmest winter boots. Then she went upstairs and arranged her sleeping bag neatly over her mat and fixed the pillow.

Back in the kitchen, Ashley asked, "Hey Nicole, what shall we have for breakfast?"

"I'm going to have some cereal and half of my orange." She took a knife out of the holder and slowly cut through the orange.

"Can I have the other half?" Ashley asked.

"Sure." She looked over at Papa sipping at his cup of coffee while scrolling over his phone screen. "Hey Papa?"

"Yes, what is it?"

"Do you think you can get Mama to make me stay home today? I still don't feel a hundred percent."

"I think not, Nicole. Come on, let's not be milking the tragedy. I'm sorry you were so sick, but that doesn't earn you an extra day off."

"Okay, okay." She looked at her sister and could see that Ashley already had a hunch about what was on her mind. She had that knowing kid sister look all about her.

"Now you girls have a wonderful day and I'll see

you at dinner time," Papa said as he put on his wool overcoat and left. They could hear his car starting up and driving away.

Ashley whispered, "Are you skipping?"

Nicole made a zipper motion across her lips. She eyed Ashley and gave a slight nod.

Ashley nodded back. They finished their breakfast in silence and brought their used plates and glasses to the sink.

❧ 10 ❧

Alpine Adventure

NICOLE FELT AN uncustomary sense of loneliness
when Ashley ran off for the tram to Innsbruck. Normally she didn't miss her sister for a simple school
day, but the image of Ashley with her curly golden
head tossed back in the throes of a laughing fit, and
that moment of conspiracy between them at breakfast
made her feel a closeness that stayed in her mind. She
walked through Gartendorf and stopped at the maga-
zine store while waiting for the later tram. Finally it
arrived, and there were only a dozen or so passengers,
all adults. Mr. Engle was not driving. Nicole sat in a
seat and took a slow, deep breath.

She knew that she had to get off at the Old Town
stop before the bridge, to make sure she wouldn't be

seen by any school stragglers. The last thing she needed was some busybody making noise about her being seen on the way to school but missing from classes. When she got off the tram, the winter air pinched at her nose. Her breath came in steamy puffs. She lifted her school sack over her back and walked down toward the bridge. She could see Boznik's market stall on the other side. No matter how much she thought about what to say, she couldn't shake her disappointment with the candy cane and the promise of magic. The amazement she had felt when she first tasted the candy cane was almost dissolved.

Boznik was smiling when she arrived. "So, my young friend!" he said. "No school today?"

"I'm supposed to be in school."

"You have something more important, I gather?"

Nicole came very close and unhitched her school sack, put it on the cobblestone pavement in front of her feet. She opened the zipper and pulled out the candy cane. "It was a nice story and all, but I think I need to give back the candy cane," she said, shaking her head. "There's no magic."

He held open his hand with the Aztec sun tattoo on the palm. "Do you really think so?"

She nodded, suddenly feeling very sad. Tears came to her eyes as she handed him the candy cane, and she could feel the tears turn cold as they trickled over her cheeks.

He looked at her with a concerned pout, and tugged on his chin beard with his free hand. He put the candy cane up to his ear as if to listen to it.

"My dear friend," he said. "This candy cane tells me that you have had more magic than most. Just because you don't recognize magic doesn't mean it is not there."

"Everybody has good and bad in their life," she said. "I think mostly bad things have happened since I took the candy cane."

"Come now, open those eyes!" he said. "You may not be standing here today if not for the magic."

She wiped her eyes and looked at him. "What do you mean by that?"

Boznik closed his eyes and turned his head upward while making a dramatic spiral in the air with his fingers. "I see snow. . .You are eating snow. Tell me about it."

"Lots of people like to eat snow," she said. She suspected he was playing the fortune teller, trying to divine somebody's life by guessing at a common activity. How else could he know what she did days ago?

"What were you doing when you were eating the snow?"

Nicole shrugged. "Just skiing with my sister. We were going along the trails behind our house. I stopped to eat snow because Ashley was going a little slow and I wanted her to catch up."

"And did something happen?"

"Yes. I was hit by a golf ball."

Boznik opened his eyes and looked directly at Nicole. "In the head?"

She suddenly realized what Boznik was getting at, and felt a rush of heat through her body. "No, on my — my — leg."

"Ahh! . . . a reasonable price to pay for your brains, no?"

She shuddered, remembering very clearly the first golf ball that whizzed in front of her face and made her almost keel over. She never could have thought of her injury as being some sort of heavenly gift. "But —"

"So what was that you were saying about there being no magic?" he said. He waved the candy cane in front of his face. "I smell fire. What about fire? I see a house in a mountain village —"

Nicole covered her ears with both hands. "Stop! I don't want to talk about it!" she cried. She could feel her heart pounding. How could he know these things?

Boznik stood still, looking into her eyes. A very gentle smile crossed his face, and he dropped into a crouch so he could be face-to-face with her. She slowly took her hands down from her ears.

"This isn't about the candy cane," he said. "It's about the magic. The hand of God is very powerful, but sometimes very quiet."

Nicole took a deep, staggering breath of the icy air. "I thought you said it was a magic candy cane."

"Well, I did. But the candy cane is not the magic any more than the antenna is the broadcast, the trumpet is the music, the book is the knowledge, or the telephone is the conversation. Some people go around looking for miracles as if God is going to hang a sign on every gift. I think you already know that you've seen a lot of magic that you just haven't realized was magic. Think about it. You're very smart. Tell me three bits of magic since you last came here."

For a moment Nicole was annoyed. This was much harder than school. She came to return the candy cane to Boznik, plain and simple, but now found herself playing quiz games. But from her annoyance arose the image of Marcel Bouchon and his magnificently crafted Advent calendar.

"Wow," she said, feeling a smile growing almost unwanted on her face. "Mr. Bouchon made something a long time ago to give to his little boy. There was a horrible car accident and his wife and little boy died. The other day he said he was giving it to my sister and me to keep."

"Hmm," Boznik said. He stroked his chin beard, twirling it in his hand. "That's one. Now two more."

"Okay. My mother was really worried after the fire because the fire inspector told her she couldn't use any food in the house because of smoke. Then

Grandpa and Grandma just showed up and brought a chicken dinner."

Boznik nodded, still looking into Nicole's eyes.

"And I'm going to get a new cousin!" she said, now feeling the smile grow across her face. "Uncle Johan and his girlfriend Pascale are coming for Christmas, and she's going to have a baby in spring. And plus, the other night I saw a snowstorm out the window that was snowing only on the left while the moon was shining on the right. Then —"

"Aha! Now you see?" Boznik said as he stood back up and handed Nicole the candy cane. "Magic everywhere! Heaven intersects Earth all the time, otherwise how could we possibly recognize Heaven when we finally get there? It doesn't mean there will be no trouble in your days, but if you see the magic it will make the trouble less."

Nicole took the candy cane and hugged it to her chest. "Speaking of trouble, I'm going to get my own personal taste of it for skipping school."

"Trouble makes life interesting," he said, fiddling with an earring. "It's not a problem — it's a challenge. If it's a problem, it's on top of you. If it's a challenge, you're on top of it."

❦ ❋ ❧

NICOLE TUCKED THE candy cane into her school sack and waved to Boznik as snow began to fall. She was glad she dressed warmly, because now she had the rest of the day to herself. She thought it might be fun to go window shopping through the city while Max Brunheim squirmed in his place next to her empty seat at school. But the chance of being seen by somebody who might know her parents was high, especially during the holiday shopping season. Seeing a movie would have been a good way to pass some time until school was over, but she hadn't thought to take the ten euros with her. She wanted to save all her money to get her own phone, and up until now, that seemed most important. She also realized that she had forgotten to pack her lunch. All the time she kept after Ashley to remember her lunch, and here she was forgetting her own. She would have to have the Saint Nicholas chocolates and let that do until she got home.

She walked to the edge of the city where the foothills began, and found an old hiking road that would lead her above the rooftops. Hiking in the flurries made her feel like she was inside a great big snow globe, and she could watch the trees and the whole world around her turn into a soft wonderland. She liked the sense of flight she got when she was high enough to see the buildings, roads and river stretching out below her. She caught snowflakes in her gloves, and inspected them to see their infinite variations.

There was so much to think about. She continued walking uphill for what seemed like hours, enjoying the fresh snowfall as it sifted through the trees and made gentle whispering sounds in the branches. She thought about Papa's story of the American student who traveled the whole wide world tasting snow. It would be something if snow really could taste like chocolate. She took her school sack off her shoulders and unzipped the pocket, and took out two Saint Nicholas pieces. The snow was now covering the ground, and beginning to fall faster. It could only be better if she had her cross-country skis with her. She put the school sack back on her shoulders and clumsily peeled the foil off the chocolate with her gloves. A sudden breeze blew snow into her face and snatched the foil away. She tried to catch it, but it was out of sight quickly.

She took a bite of the chocolate, then opened her mouth to let more snow blow in. Real chocolate snow — and she wasn't even in Switzerland. Another gust came and shifted her hat, and snow blew into her ear. She turned opposite the wind and pulled the hat back on more securely. Her view of the city below was now obscured, and it seemed that the snowfall was turning into a storm. It would be wise to start back down.

There would be plenty enough of Innsbruck for her to explore without going into the shopping districts. She finished the second chocolate as she followed her footprints back downhill. In a few minutes she came to a dead end, realizing the new snow had erased all signs of her passage. She would have to guess her way down.

A short distance later she was unexpectedly whipped back by a fierce blast of wind that stung her face and took her breath away. Snow blown up the nose did not taste good in any country. Wind continued to buffet her from all sides, and no way that she turned was protected. Where did this squall come from? She couldn't see which direction she was moving, and trying to stay still was futile. She was being swept into a mountain blizzard.

She could make out a grove of pines nearby, and did her best to forge her way toward them. They were leaning hard in the relentless gust, and just as she was close enough to grab a branch, another twist of wind swiped at her from a different direction and drove her to the ground. She could feel herself actually blowing away, all 35 kilograms plus school sack turning into a wind-propelled human toboggan with a smooth ski coat front for the glide. It was almost fun, except that she had no idea where the ride might stop. Would she slam into a rock? Get blown off a cliff? She couldn't see where she was going. Snow was coming down like the storied snows of Perm, centimeters at a time and all at once. She could make out a dark form, then another, as she swooped helplessly across the hill past some trees.

She scrambled as best she could, kicking her feet and flailing her arms to try to grab some ground to hold. The snow was filling her eyes and melting down her neck. She began to panic that she would drown in the snow, and prayed with all her heart for an angel's protection. The wind continued to buffet her face as it howled over the landscape. Her cheeks were numb and her eyelids were beginning to freeze. She wanted to wipe them with the backs of her gloves, but she needed her hands and feet for any chance she might get to grab something, anything, that might stop her from being blown away like a leaf in a hurricane.

At last she plunged sideways into a huge snow-drift. The sudden stop yanked the school sack down into her shoulders, making her head fling back. She grabbed the snowdrift and dug into it with hands and feet, crawling until she could feel the spinning world slow down. She kept crawling until she bumped her head into a tree trunk. "A tree!" she cried soundlessly in the howling wind. "Thank you, thank you."

Somehow she got herself onto the quiet side of the tall pine. She pulled off a glove and covered her eyes with a warm hand, wiping away the frost that glued her eyelashes. She could see just enough to know that she was in a small outcropping of pine trees. Where the snow had not been funneled away by the wind, she could see that it was more than knee-deep.

She knew she was in trouble now. With snow this deep, she would never be able to make it back into the city before sundown, even if she could figure out which way it was, even if the blizzard stopped now. If she stepped out of the trees, she would be whipped back into the wind. If she stayed where she was, she realized that she could very easily freeze to death as those two mountain climbers did last winter.

Her stomach began to grow tense as she tried to imagine what she might do to keep herself safe and alive. She looked up into the branches and saw that they were laden with snow. Somehow the wind had not been as strong inside the grove of pines. Maybe there was a cliff nearby that stopped the wind? Could there be a cave or sheltering boulder where she could hide from the storm? She would have to do something besides just sitting under a pine tree if she didn't want to be found frozen stiff and buried under the snow.

She felt a paralyzing fear creeping into her chest and stomach. Breathe, breathe, she thought. Don't panic. Panic is the enemy. She turned her thoughts toward things she learned in Girl Guides, school, and karate class that might be useful while stranded all alone in a mountain blizzard. One thing she did know: never go wandering once you've lost your direction. Papa had told her many times on their hikes that unless you have a road or direction, wandering will only make you go in circles and tire you out. Better to stay in one place until you can figure out north, south, east and west.

At least she wasn't very cold except where snow had sneaked inside her clothing. Her hands and feet were still okay, although she was beginning to feel very thirsty. She picked up a pile of snow and looked at it in her glove. A taste with her tongue made her think of her grandfather's story of the American soldier and his lemon snow. Maybe she could be like that American soldier, who hid away from the enemy in snowdrifts until he could get back to safety. She ate all of the snow in her glove, then had another handful. The thought of lemon sweetness made her taste it in the snow, and she found herself smiling. She thought of what Boznik had told her. It's not a problem, it's a challenge. If it's a problem, it's on top of you. If it's a challenge, you're on top of it.

She had camped out in the cold before. Sure, she had used an insulated sleeping bag and wasn't lying down on snow. And there were other people with her. Here in the hills outside the city, she could be alone for days before anybody found her. And she had no food but a few more pieces of Saint Nicholas chocolate and a candy cane. The snowstorm continued to howl all around. Now and then a blast of wind would toss the upper branches of the pines above her, dumping snow helter-skelter.

How long had she been up here? It seemed the sky was darkening, though she thought it was only midafternoon. She was beginning to grow hungry. Very hungry. And she would need to get some shelter before dark, or else she would be groping around in hurricane winds to find a cave or stone crevice to crawl into. Carefully she moved into a crawling position, newly feeling the pain of her golf ball injury as she slowly made her way to the next pine tree. Again the wind tossed the boughs, and a small avalanche of tree snow dropped heavily onto her. Some went down the back of her neck and she brushed away as much of it as she could, but the damage was done. The snow melted and trickled down her back and chilled her to the core.

There was only one thing left to try. She thought about Professor Nicolosantapopov and his students stuck for three days on the old bus in Perm. The snow would insulate, and could be used for shelter if she started building right now while it was still light enough to see what she was doing. She remembered last winter when she and Ashley built a snow fort with Max Brunheim. She quickly began to scoop the snow together and found it was good snowman material. Heavy, not too dry. She crawled back to the first pine tree she had found, on the protected side. She began scooping the snow together and shaping it into blocks. One block on top of the other, she formed slightly leaning walls that came as high as her waist, one on the left of the tree trunk and one on the right, with the tree for the back wall. There had to be a small doorway for her to crawl into, and that would be on the down side of the wind. She kept working until the walls were built.

Now she had to get a roof on the shelter, and she hoped the snow would stay where she put it. She knelt inside the shelter and carefully formed an arched area against the wide trunk, pressing and patting the snow until she had the beginning shape of the igloo roof outlined against the tree. The snow inside her shelter floor was pressed smooth and hard from all the building, and she had to venture into the clearing to supply more snow.

Twilight fell before she was finished with the shelter. The front part of the roof caved in when she was pressing snow on top, and she had to rebuild it two times before it held together. She patted it smooth from the inside to make sure there were no weak spots. Finally she packed more snow on the roof to get more insulation.

There was a sudden smell of cows on the wind, just a hint that came and went. It made her wonder how close any farm might be. She took her hat off and banged the snow off against her leg, then put the hat back on. She crawled inside the shelter and hoped that she would begin to feel warmer. Her feet were cold, and her hands were wet through her gloves. But the howling wind was blockaded, and the inside of her little igloo was as quiet as could be. It was big enough for her to kneel and move around in.

She knew she would have to stay the night, and she would have to be at least warm enough not to freeze. She yanked off her gloves and opened her school sack. She rummaged inside and found her extra pair of thermal socks, then felt inside the pocket for her hand warmers. She found three more foil-wrapped Saint Nicholas chocolates along with her candy cane.

One at a time she pulled off her boots, and gently rolled off the socks. They were damp in the toes. She pulled on the dry socks and quickly put her feet back into the boots before they could get cold. Then came the part she never did before, but heard about so many times from Grandpa. When he was in the Ardennes Forest during the war, he kept an extra pair of socks with him all the time. He would wear one pair on his feet and the other pair across his chest, to keep them warm and dry. She unzipped her coat and lifted up her top shirt, placing the socks across her thermal ski shirt, then she tucked the top shirt back into her pants. Wiggling her toes fast made her feet feel better as she ripped open her first hand warmer packet and shook it in the air to activate it. She held it until it reached full heat, almost too hot to keep holding. It would last for ten hours.

She pulled off her hat and put the warmer into it, then put it over her face to breathe the heated air. It was going to be a long, long night. She knew that her father and mother would be out searching for her. How could she end up lost like this in a mountain blizzard, when all she wanted to do was take an ordinary hike till school was out? All that effort to punish the Brunheim boys and keep from getting caught skipping school, and now she was as caught as she could be. Police would be out looking for her, and they would find out right away that she had never stepped foot into school. Boznik was the last person to see her, but what could he tell anybody of Nicole's whereabouts? Sooner or later Ashley would have to admit she knew Nicole was skipping. The last time a child went missing in the mountains, nearly two hundred people turned out to help find him. But that was not in a blinding mountain blizzard.

And what if there were any hungry animals prowling for food? The thought of that intensified her need to pee, and she knew she would never be able to hold it till the morning. She stuck the hat on top of her head again and pulled on her gloves. She shimmied backwards out of the shelter and crawled over to the next pine tree. She braced herself for the rush of cold on her bare skin as she performed the camper's necessity with incredible speed, then hustled back into her igloo just in time to pull her hat back off. The hand warmer was getting too hot. And her wet gloves were too cold to keep wearing, so she tugged them off.

Now very hungry, she ate the last pieces of chocolate she could find. Then she curled up on the snow floor and rested her head on her school sack with her hat perched over her face. At least she would have warm air to breathe, and one more hand warmer in case things got any worse later on. She pulled her arms all the way up her coat sleeves, folding them across her body and tucking her fingers under her armpits.

She tried to stay awake, reciting as many poems and prayers as she could remember. She thought of Ashley, and wished that she could be home with her, trying out their new fingernail polish together. Soon the hard packed snow beneath her faded from sensation and she felt her body drifting into slumber.

❀ 11 ❀

The Morning After

WHEN NICOLE WOKE up she had the strange sensation of something stirring against her. She thought the igloo roof had caved in, but the scant light through the crooked doorway showed the roof was still intact. She felt something moving again and she became wide awake with fear, thinking a mountain animal had come in. She took a deep breath and smelled dog.

"Fang! You came to find me," she said. She wriggled her arms into the cold sleeves of her coat. "How did you get all the way up here?"

He seemed very quiet. She realized that he had been sleeping snuggled close to her, because she was not especially cold except for her face and her toes. She hugged him, and saw that her hand warmer was on the floor in a rectangular hole in the snow, and her hat was on her school sack.

Blitzen shuffled outside the igloo and Nicole watched him shake himself, his tail arching in a left curl. He barked into the igloo.

"Okay, Fang, I'm coming," she said. She put her hat on, pulling it tight over her ears. As she changed position she could feel the extra pair of socks jumbled around her waistline. She gathered her school sack and gloves, then crawled out into the morning sunrise. Pink clouds dotted the clearing sky, and from the look of the mountains she thought she may have hiked here in better weather.

The snow lay in sweeping drifts up to her knees all around, but not in front of her igloo door or on the lee side of the surrounding pine trees. She was pleased with herself that she had built down from the wind.

She sat in front of her igloo and unzipped her ski coat, pulled up her shirt and tugged out the pair of socks. Sure enough, they were dry and somewhat warm. A shiver went through her as she took off her boots. As soon as she doubled up the first sock, she pushed her foot back into the boot, then hurried on with the other. Then she pulled on her frosted gloves, working her fingers to get full motion.

Blitzen nuzzled her leg and whimpered, and began to walk ahead through the snow. Nicole knew he must have struggled through snow drifts and wind-blown terrain to reach her, a very hard journey for a farm dog. She could not imagine how he could have found her, or what he could possibly be doing away from the Brunheim Farm. He kept turning back to ensure that she was following him.

They continued through the snow until the city came into view. It seemed a kilometer away, but there it was in bright morning light. A helicopter was flying in toward the hills, getting noisier as it approached. It passed in the distance, then looped around and flew along the peaks behind them.

There were long patches of bare ground that the wind carved out during the blizzard, and Nicole followed them as much as possible. She noticed that Blitzen was stopping a lot, and was shaking his paws, licking them now and then. At one point he stopped on some bare ground and lay down. Nicole knelt before him and patted his fur. She could see that his paws were cracked and frozen, and there was some blood between the pads. She pulled off her gloves and put them gently onto Blitzen's forepaws. The dog looked up to her with grateful eyes, then began to shiver all over. She had never seen a dog do that. She thought he must be overcome with cold.

She lifted off her school sack and unzipped the pocket. She took out the remaining hand warmer and sat on the ground to tear open the package. Her fingers were a little stiff, but she got it open and rubbed it between her hands in hopes of activating the heat more quickly. She pressed it against the dog's chest and rubbed in a circle. "Come now," she said. "We're almost there. When we get to the city you can get a nice hot bath and get all brushed." She continued to stroke him from his neck down his back. Again he shivered, and his eyes looked wobbly.

"I think you're sick like I was the other day," she said. She left the hand warmer on his side to pull off her boots. She took off the extra pair of thermal socks, then she crammed her feet back into her boots as fast as she could. She knelt at Blitzen's side again and fitted the socks onto his hind legs. The hand warmer slid off him, and she picked it up and pressed it back against his coat, rubbing around his neck and chest. He seemed to be resting, but after a few minutes she noticed he was peeing right where he lay, and was getting it on himself. She realized that his breathing had stopped, and he lay still with eyes half open.

She shook him gently. "Hey, Fang? Fang?"

Nothing.

She could feel her heart sink as she stood up slowly over the dog. Tears filled her eyes and blurred the image of him lying there on the frozen ground with her gloves and socks placed over his paws. She began to sob, realizing that all of this was because of her. This was not the punishment she ever would have wanted for the Brunheim boys, but it was the punishment she was delivering. She knew that she was going to get her own personal ration of trouble when she got home, and somehow she could accept it. But she could not accept that Blitzen's last moments were spent away from his happy farmhouse, coming to rescue her in a place she never should have been.

She stood crying until her throat was dry. Presently she wiped her eyes, noticing how cold her hands had become. She looked at her gloves on Blitzen, and decided that with the dog's blood and frost sores, she could not put them back on her hands. She pulled down both her coat sleeves and put each hand up the opposite sleeve, holding her hands around her forearms. Then she realized she should take the hand warmer, since it would no longer do any good for the dog. But her hands were already in her sleeves, and she was beginning to shiver badly. Better to just keep moving.

Again the helicopter flew overhead and crossed into the city. Nicole continued to walk down the hill as fast as she could go, keeping to as many windblown pathways as she could find. In some spots the snow was above her knees. As she plowed her way through, she became thirsty and pulled a hand out to gather some snow. She ate some, but the cold only made her shiver more intensely. In the next patch of visible ground she took off her school sack and found her candy cane. It was still intact after all it had been through. She peeled off the wrapper and rolled it into her pocket. Then she put the candy cane into her mouth and kept walking until she spied something shiny flickering in the snow in front of her. She bent down to pick it up.

It was the foil wrapping of the Saint Nicholas chocolate that the wind blew away yesterday. She put the foil into her pocket, and noticed that her fingers were an odd purplish color. She looked ahead to see the rooftops of city buildings just a short distance below. The helicopter was approaching again, and this time it hovered overhead, stopping in the sky above her.

BY THE TIME Nicole reached the lowest stretch of the hiking trail, the sound of sirens drowned out the hovering helicopter. She could see three Innsbruck Police wagons, a fire engine and an ambulance clustering in the roadway straight ahead. She stumbled and almost tripped over her own footsteps. Each step she took, it seemed her feet weren't completely touching the ground. She didn't want to be in trouble with the police. Perhaps they would call her mother and ask her to come. It would be nice to go home again.

She felt lightheaded and strangely warm all over as she saw more vehicles approaching. The police were getting out of their wagons and putting up their hands to stop traffic in the roadway. More police were coming with rescue dogs. A news truck parked behind the blockade, and some people jumped out and ran toward the cluster.

The police officers became blurry as they came hurrying up the hiking trail. She couldn't tell if there were three or four of them. She took the candy cane out of her mouth, and her hand seemed unable to hold it. The candy cane slipped out of her fingers onto the snow.

"Are you Nicole Kinders?"

She couldn't tell which one spoke to her. She tried to make out their faces.

"Where's Mama?" she said, and felt her knees go limp as she collapsed into somebody's arms.

❦ 12 ❧

Flowers in Winter

THE POLICE OFFICER nearest to the lost girl reached his arms out to catch her as she dropped forward. There was a flurry of movement all around as the officers with rescue dogs rushed beyond him and followed her footprints up the hiking trail. Newspeople clambered around the scene with video cameras, trying to capture close-ups of the girl in the policeman's arms. Other newspeople followed the rescue dogs.

The two uniformed women who drove the ambulance already had the rolling stretcher on the plowed roadway, and were wheeling it through icy crags to get to the girl. The police officer stepped carefully over lumps of compacted snow to bring the girl to the stretcher. He sat her down, and the first woman reached for the straps on the girl's school sack to un-hitch it from her shoulders. She pulled off the school sack and placed it at the foot of the stretcher. The second woman took hold of the girl's wrist and felt for her pulse.

"We have a female child approximate age twelve in apparent critical hypothermia," she said into a head-set microphone. "Pulse is positive, but weak and rapid. Transporting immediately to Children's Hospital."

Within a few minutes the girl was strapped onto the stretcher and whisked past news cameras into the ambulance and away, with the siren wailing its famil-iar high-low notes.

Immediately the news was broadcast that Nicole Kinders had been found. Internet, radio and televi-sion buzzed to announce that she was in an Innsbruck hospital, and that her condition was unknown. Up-dates were promised.

"Eleven-year-old Nicole Kinders was found mo-ments ago at the base of a pathway leading to the Alderweg Hiking Trail," one television announcer said. "She was reported missing during the blizzard last evening, and apparently spent the entire night outdoors. Police with rescue dogs have been follow-ing her trail in the snow, and are now scouring the mountain paths for any possible sign of other miss-ing or injured people. It is not known why Nicole was on the mountain trail, but a neighbor in Gartendorf, Konrad Brunheim, said that she may have gone there in search of his dog Blitzen, which left home during a power failure caused by yesterday's fierce blizzard conditions."

Meanwhile, Nicole's parents were rushing into Children's Hospital, breathless and exhausted after their harrowing night driving in the blizzard, calling every possible person who might know anything about where Nicole might be. Her mother's phone was out of battery power, and her father's was very low. They had left Ashley with Aunt Valeria, who was now driving her through snowy roads to the hospital instead of to school.

A doctor met with the parents as soon as they arrived. He introduced himself as Dr. Reichardt, and told them that Nicole was undergoing active rewarming, involving a combination of warming blankets and warmed intravenous fluids. He said that she was still in danger, as her core temperature had dropped to 34 degrees Celsius from the normal 37. "In addition to this," he said, "there is the issue of a significant injury to her pelvis. She may have fallen or struck something. We'd like to take X-rays to make sure no bone structures are involved."

"When can we see her?" asked her mother. "Is a priest available?"

"As soon as possible," the doctor said. "Before we go in, I need to tell you what to expect. In hypothermia, the body goes into a reserve function where blood flow is increased to the heart, brain and lungs, and cut back from the hands and feet. She had no gloves when she was found. You may be alarmed to see swelling in her fingertips. We get several cases of this each winter, and most of the time the swelling goes away without complications. In the worst case, she may need some plastic surgery on the fingers. She's a very fortunate child. She seems to be responding well to warming therapy, but she is coming in and out of consciousness."

"Please take us to her," said her father.

NICOLE BECAME AWARE of somebody's hands on her arms. Her whole body jumped, and she heard her own voice crying out, "No!" as she opened her eyes and saw her mother on one side of the hospital bed and her father on the other side, holding her wrists. "Mama," she said, and began to cry.

"Okay, sweetheart. We're here, we're right here." Mama put her face close, and kissed Nicole again and again. "We're so glad to have you back. The priest was here a few minutes ago to anoint you."

"I'm sorry, Mama."

"Shhh. Whatever happened, you don't need to worry. We can talk about it later if you need to. Just get better so you can come home."

"I was having a horrible dream. Will they have to cut off my fingers?"

"Absolutely not," Papa said.

"You're going to be fine," Mama said, "although I wouldn't recommend clapping your hands for a couple of days."

"When can I come home?"

"Well, hopefully tomorrow," she said. "We have to see what Dr. Reichardt says."

At that moment Ashley plunged into the room, followed by Aunt Valeria. "Hey Nicole! You're completely famous," Ashley said. "You were on every station on Aunty's backseat video." She came up to the bed and reached her hand out to touch Nicole. "Oh my gosh, your fingers look like grapes." She shuddered.

Aunt Valeria stood back with her hand over her mouth. She was trembling, looking horrified.

"I think I'm okay," Nicole said. "But I'm really hungry."

"I've been saying prayers nonstop since last night," Aunt Valeria said. "I'm going to have a head full of gray hair before Christmas."

There was a knock at the door, and a nurse brought in a floral arrangement of red and white roses mixed with holly and boxwood. "This is for Nicole," she said. "It says, 'Get back on your feet real soon! Innsbruck Police Department.' You have about fifteen more deliveries, honey. Looks like you're Miss Popular today."

"Is it okay if I have something to eat?" Nicole said.

"Of course you may," the nurse said. "Is there anything special you'd like?"

"Some cereal with milk, please. And some hot chocolate?"

"I think we can have that brought in," she said. "Now I'll get your other deliveries."

The nurse came back with two other nurses, all of them carrying flower arrangements. They went back and forth three times and crowded the windowsill and the floor in front of it with flowers and gifts. Ashley went over and began to read each greeting. "This one is from your class at school, this one is from Uncle Johan and Pascale. The next is from Girl Guides Troop 6020, and one from Landmark Realty, and this one is from Importazioni di Benevento. Did I say that right?"

"Perfetto," said Aunt Valeria.

"This one has a little horse made of straw. It says, 'Get well soon! Cementa of Sweden.' Who's that?"

"Ah, Erik!" Papa said. "That's not a horse. It's a goat, a Julbock, they call it. They're our supplier of concrete for the new warehouse in Malmo." He rubbed his eyes and yawned. "We'll have a lot of thank-you notes to write. When your fingers are better, of course."

"Can we get some nice cards at the store?" Nicole asked.

"Let's get you home first," Mama said. "Hopefully we can go shopping on Saturday, and we can get our new Christmas tree, too."

An orderly walked into the room with a tray of food and a white box wrapped in a bright green ribbon. He placed them on the bedside cart and said, "This just arrived, from Zimt & Zucker Bakery. Six warm apple fritters, just for you."

"Oh, thank you so much!" Nicole said. "I'll really enjoy that."

After the orderly left, Mama said, "Let's just let Nicole have her breakfast. Do you want me to help you with the cereal, sweetie?"

"I think I can do it," Nicole said. "Should we turn on the television?"

"If you'd like," Papa said. "Let's open up that box of apple fritters. I may like one of those myself."

Another knock at the doorway, and Marcel Bouchon peeked in. He was holding one hand behind his back. "Is it okay for me to enter?"

Mama said, "Please do, Mr. Bouchon. Thank you so much for coming."

He walked up to Nicole and reached out his free hand to touch her chin. "Last night when I heard you were lost, I asked my little Roger to watch over you. It looks like you're going to be as good as new." He took his hand from behind his back and showed Nicole two stuffed teddy bears with the plushest velveteen fur, one white and the other black. "I didn't know what color you would like, so I got both," he said.

"Oh, they're so cute!" she said. "I think I want the black one. Is it okay if I give the other one to Ashley?"

"Well, that's just what I was going to recommend,"

he said. "Now I'd love to stay, but I have much work to do today and you have to have your breakfast."

"Mr. Bouchon?"

"Yes, Nicole."

"You didn't put up the Advent calendar yet, did you?"

"No, no — that I can only do when you girls are both home."

"Okay. Thanks so much for my teddy bear! I really love it. I can't wait to hold him."

"Me too, Mr. Bouchon," Ashley said. "Thank you. And I hope you'll come to our house for Christmas Eve, because everybody will be there."

"Oh, I'll see you before that," he said. He turned and almost bumped into Aunt Valeria. "Excuse me, mademoiselle." He put his hand on her arm, and she looked down at it, blinking her eyes. "May I interest you in dinner in the Old Town Saturday evening?" he asked. "I know a lovely little place that looks out over the Christmas Market."

"That sounds absolutely divine," she said, putting her hand on his. "What time shall I be ready?"

"Will five o'clock be good?"

"Short of any other disasters, it should be perfect."

When Marcel Bouchon left the room, Mama untied the ribbon on the bakery box and lifted out an apple fritter to put on Nicole's tray. Nicole clumsily picked it up and began eating. "Oh, it's sooo good! I've never been so hungry in all my life." Then she tried to maneuver her cereal spoon to her mouth without using her swollen fingertips, but it was too difficult. "Mama, I think I'll need you to help me. I feel like such a big baby."

"Don't you worry, I'm glad to help. Do you want some of your hot chocolate?"

"Okay, just use the spoon. I'm afraid to spill it."

Papa picked up the remote control for the overhead television set and turned it on. He flicked through a few stations and stopped at a news broadcast that flashed a banner, "Nicole Kinders Found Wednesday AM."

" . . . and police with rescue dogs discovered a sad scene in the hills above Innsbruck," the announcer said. "Apparently an Austrian Pinscher had escaped his radio fencing when power was interrupted during yesterday's intense blizzard. The dog, named Blitzen, was found by eleven-year-old neighbor Nicole Kinders. Amazingly, as you can see, Nicole used her best skills to survive while stranded overnight in the blizzard. She built this compact igloo against the trunk of a pine tree with her own hands. This morning, in her attempt to lead Blitzen to safety in frigid conditions, Nicole heroically sacrificed some of her clothing to save the dog, but unfortunately the dog did not survive. Blitzen's body was found with Nicole's gloves and socks placed over his paws, and a hand warmer that was still warm, over his heart. Now Nicole's life is in grave danger because of her sacrifice. A search helicopter spotted her at seven-twenty-two this morning, and a team of Innsbruck police rushed to meet her at the base of a hiking trail. She collapsed from hypothermia and was immediately taken to Children's Hospital, where her condition remains critical. Konrad Brunheim of the Brunheim Farm in Gartendorf said that he was not surprised that Nicole Kinders would fight a blizzard in search of his family's dog. 'She's a very special girl, and I hope she will be all right,' Brunheim said."

Aunt Valeria had tears in her eyes. "Oh, my poor niece," she said. "You went through hell."

"I think they made up some of the story," Nicole said. "It's not exactly the way it happened."

"How did it happen?" Ashley asked. She placed her hand on Nicole's leg and squeezed lightly. "You'll have to tell us *everything.*"

Nicole could see that look again in Ashley's eyes, that same look she saw across the table at breakfast yesterday. Somehow with that one word, Ashley affirmed that nothing of Nicole's secrets had yet been told. "I promise I'll tell you, okay?" Nicole said. "Just not right now."

"I'm very impressed with the igloo," Papa said. "Where, pray tell, did you ever come up with that idea?"

"From you, Papa. Don't you remember your story about the Russian snow? You said the snow helped to insulate the old broken-down school bus, but not as good as an igloo."

"Ah, so I did," he said. "And my daughter has an astonishing retention of my stories! Tell me, did the igloo work?"

"It helped, but it was still bitter cold. I don't know if I would have made it through the night without —"

The nurse stepped into the room with a small gift box. She brought it to Nicole and said, "Sorry to interrupt, but this was just delivered for you."

"Thank you," Nicole said. "Does it say who sent it?"

"No, it says just 'Nicole,' nothing else."

"Shall I open it for you?" Ashley asked.

"Okay, open it." Nicole watched as Ashley took the crimson satin ribbon off the slim box. She opened it to show a single candy cane. There was no message, but there didn't need to be any. Nicole knew exactly where it had come from.

❧ 13 ❧

A Cup of Good Cheer

AFTER NEARLY THREE days in the Innsbruck Children's Hospital, Nicole was finally allowed to go home. Her room in the hospital had become crammed with gifts and flowers from friends and strangers all over the world. Her name had the most hits on Google for that Wednesday, and by Thursday the news footage of her igloo was played over a million times on YouTube. Before leaving the hospital Friday, Nicole helped her parents select which of the gifts would go home, and which of them she wanted to donate. There were enough toys, dolls and books for every child in the hospital, and enough flowers for all who would be able to enjoy them.

Saturday morning Nicole woke up in her own bed, in her own flannel pajamas, with her new black velveteen teddy bear. No more needles stuck in her arms, no more X-ray machines, no more thick gauze wraps around her fingers. She stretched as far as her arms could go, and then turned her fingers forward so she could look at them in the early morning light. Only her two middle fingers still had bandages. It was so good to be home again. But she was not as happy as she would wish to be. Blitzen weighed heavily on her mind, and she felt horrible that everybody thought she had gone looking for the dog in the blizzard when, in fact, it was the other way around. From the news stories, she discovered that her igloo was less than one kilometer beyond the end of the Brunheim Farm road. No wonder she smelled cows during the blizzard. To think that she could have died less than two kilometers from her own front door was disturbing.

She went into the bathroom and sat for a long time staring at the tile floor, watching the patterns transform again and again. Then she pulled off her finger bandages and washed her hands. The skin of her fingertips seemed to be healing nicely. When the water became a little warmer, she splashed her face.

She shut off the water and heard strange sounds coming from the back porch. Probably an animal, she thought. In fall a chamois had come into the yard and clambered across the porch. Mama found it nibbling on Nicole's hiking shoe, and ran to get her phone for a picture, but when she returned the chamois was gone.

Nicole tiptoed out of the bathroom and looked at Ashley's bedroom door. It was still closed. There was a soft tap-tap-tap on the back door. Definitely not the sound of a chamois. Nicole frowned, wondering who would be calling so early in the morning, and at the back door no less. She eased open the door and came face-to-face with Max Brunheim. She gasped. Max looked at the floor.

Her first instinct was to slam the door, but looking at him standing there with a black eye and stitches in his eyebrow, she thought she should give him a chance to speak. She took a few steps backwards and put her finger up to her lips, then motioned him in. He pulled off his boots at the door, and she led him to the parlor. "What's this about?" she said.

Max was still looking at the floor. "I just wanted to thank you for trying to save Blitzen," he said.

"Did your Papa make you come here?"

"No. I just got done feeding the cows and Papa's horse. My brothers told me you were home from the hospital. I wanted to come —" He stopped.

"Do you want to sit down?"

He shook his head and looked toward the door. For a second he glanced up at Nicole, then looked down again.

Nicole said, "I'm very sorry about your dog. He was

very brave. Everybody says I went looking for him, but that's not the truth. The real truth is that I didn't want to go to school. I skipped, because I wanted you to believe I was in the hospital from being hit by one of your wild golf balls. I was just out for a hike that day, and the blizzard caught me by surprise. I had to make a shelter, and hid inside all night. I would have frozen to death if Blitzen didn't come along. I don't know how he found me. He curled up next to me to keep me warm while I slept."

A tear splashed on the wood floor. Max lifted his head and wiped his eyes with the back of his hands, and sniffled. "I'm sorry about the golf ball, Nicole. I didn't mean to hurt you."

"I think you did mean to, Max," she said. "My sister told me that you said you were aiming at tourists. But you must have known it was my sister and me, because I was wearing my bright ski coat that you teased me about almost every day, and my sister was wearing her crazy ski hat with all the springs on it, that you were playing with. So how could you not see who it was from where you stood on the hill? I think you were mad at Isabelle Schubert. You were mad at her because she said those things in front of everybody, and you took it out on me."

Max took a deep breath. "I really didn't know it was you at first," he said, and looked into her eyes. "My brothers and I were trying to see who could hit the farthest, and then we saw two people skiing out on the trail. We should have stopped, but we didn't. Stefan was bragging that he was hitting the best, so we hit a few more. Then Andreas said he wanted to turn off the dog fence and let Blitzen go, but I thought I heard Ashley's voice yell something about golf balls. I turned around to tell him, and the next thing I knew I was on the ground with blood pouring down my eye and the sky spinning all around."

"Did he hit you on purpose?"

"No, I just turned into Stefan's backswing. When your sister told me what happened to you, I got sick to my stomach. I had no dinner on Saint Nicholas Eve. Last night I had a dream that I came here with your mother's meat order, and your house was empty. I have a stomach ache right now."

"Did you know you just missed my head by a fraction, Max? And I could have been dead on the spot?"

He shook his head. "No, I didn't."

"Well, that's exactly what happened. It almost knocked me over. I bent down to fix my ski pants and then —" Nicole turned sideways and pulled the edge of her pajama pants down to show him the purple bruise. "Then I got this."

Max took a step back and looked at her in speechless astonishment. His mouth and eyes were wide open. "I — I —"

"Right, you thought you hit me in the stomach and caused internal bleeding." She hitched her pajamas back up again. "Ashley made that whole thing up."

"I can't believe you just did that, Nicole."

She moved closer to Max. "Well, believe it. You actually caused a hairline fracture in my pelvis. The X-ray showed it at the hospital. Everybody thinks that also happened in the blizzard."

"I'm really sorry about what I did. I don't know what else to say. I was thoughtless and dumb."

"And mean, too," she said. "Don't ever be mean, Max. It's unbecoming of you. Besides, if you ever do anything to hurt me or my sister again, I'm going to invent my own karate chop and peel you like a banana." She made circles with her fingers around her eyes and stood up and down on her tiptoes. "Is that clear as mud, Max Brunheim? Clear as mud?"

He was biting his lip, but could not hold back a smile. He nodded. "I promise. I better go now, my mother will have breakfast ready soon. Please don't tell my father what happened."

She led him to the door. "Nobody knows but us kids, and I'd prefer to keep it that way. At least for now." She watched him put his boots back on, then stood in the open doorway as he ran toward home. She closed the door quickly against the chill. When she turned, Ashley was coming out of her room. "Hey, Ashley. You'll never guess what just happened."

"Wait, let me guess — Max Brunheim came? And you took him in and chewed him all up in little pieces. And then you turned around and showed him your own personal Nature Channel."

"Ashley! You were snooping?"

"I saw and heard the whole thing, Nicole. You don't think I'd sleep through that, do you? It could only have been better if you started yodeling."

"Ashley, you're such a brat. And a troublemaker."

"Oh, sure. Me, a troublemaker? You just won the World Cup."

"Shut u-up," Nicole said. "Come now, we better get ready. We have our classes today, and then we're going Christmas shopping the whole rest of the day."

❦

EVERY VOICE, EVERY touch, every sight was a pleasure to Nicole that day, as if she were discovering each ordinary thing for the very first time. When she sat down to lunch, her simple bowl of vegetable soup tasted like all of summertime. Some spice gumdrops Ashley shared with her were so strong they made both girls sneeze, so they ate more until sneezing and laughter were hard to tell apart. Mama didn't seem to be annoyed. She just smiled and handed them tissues.

Afterwards Papa drove to the tree farm, and they all searched through the rows of trees. Mama and Papa were holding hands. Finally they decided on one Tannenbaum that was as fragrant and full as a tree could possibly be. Everybody had sap on their hands except Nicole, who had it on her gloves. She needed to be careful of her fingers for a few days more. Papa tied the tree down extra tight on top of his car, and quickly found his way home. Into the stand went the new tree, placed like something royal in front of the picture window.

"Okay," Papa said. "Now let's give the tree time to settle so we can get the lights on tonight. We'll wash the sap off our hands and do some shopping."

They stopped at a stationery store and bought three different boxes of thank-you notes, two boxes of Christmas cards, some colored pens, and some Christmas paper for the printer.

"Papa?" Nicole said when they were back in the car.

"Yes, Nicole?"

"This is very important, okay?"

"I'm listening."

"We have to stop at Boznik's. I got something there last week and didn't pay for it yet."

"It's a candy cane," Ashley said. "Boznik has magic candy canes."

"Really?" Mama said. "What's so magic about them?"

"Well, mostly it's the flavor," Nicole said. "They can make you think you're tasting snow, or the wind."

"Now that's very intriguing. How much do you owe?"

"Half a euro."

"Hmm. Do you think we should get some more of these candy canes?" Mama said.

"Well, Mama — we do need to get a bunch for decorating the Christmas tree."

"Boznik is on the far side of the Old Town," Papa said. "But if it's important to you, we'll go there." He drove into the city along the tram route toward school. Just before the bridge, he found a parking spot and eased the car in. "Shall we all go?"

"Yes, let's," Mama said.

Boznik was busy with Saturday customers. People were buying oranges and apples by the sack, foil-wrapped chocolates, Linzer pigs, Almdudler sodas, key chains and batteries for cameras. When he saw Nicole approaching, Boznik stood straight up and held out both his arms. "My friend!" he said. "I see you've come back twice as hearty, twice as strong!"

Nicole ran up to Boznik and hugged him. "Thank you so much for sending me the candy cane in the hospital. This is my Papa and Mama, and you know Ashley. We came to get more candy canes."

"We hear you have magic candy canes," Papa said.

"I've been selling a lot of them today," Boznik said. "How many do you want?"

"All of them!" Nicole said.

"Just a minute, I'll have to count them." Boznik reached into a bin and took out a glass jar filled with candy canes. He lifted the bunch of them out with both hands and laid them on the counter. "Twenty-nine left," he said.

"Well, I owe you for the one you gave me last week, so that makes thirty. It should be fifteen euros."

"Yes, but you get a volume discount. Twelve euros and they're yours."

Other customers who were hovering around the market stall perked up. One said, "I'd like one of those!" Others looked upset that there wouldn't be any left.

Papa paid Boznik, and waited for him to place the candy canes into a brown paper sack. He took the sack and reached inside, then pulled out a candy cane. He handed it to one of Boznik's customers and said, "Enjoy the magic. Anybody else?"

Two other customers held out their hands.

Papa handed the sack to Nicole. She looked up at him and shrugged, then she reached into the sack and took out more candy canes. "Here you go," she said. "And for you. And you."

Boznik folded his arms and smiled his crooked smile, looking like some sort of genie just out of a magic lamp. "The magic will be revealed," he said.

By the time they got back to the car, there were only eight candy canes left. "I think we gave too many of them away," Ashley said. "We won't have enough for our tree."

"Of course we will," Nicole said. "Remember, all the ones that aren't on the tree will be making magic somewhere."

Ashley reached over and held Nicole's hand. "You

know, I didn't even think of that. Just imagine. I think we're going to have the best Christmas tree ever."

THERE WAS NOTHING quite like the Christmas Market in the Old Town of Innsbruck. Shops and stalls were decorated with abundant greenery and bows, and were full of festive gifts, ornaments and foods. Here a vendor roasted almonds and chestnuts in a wheeled cart, and there a Saint Nicholas figure played on an antique hurdy-gurdy. The roadway was paved in square cobblestones, set into circular swirl patterns as far as the eye could see. Snow-covered mountains stood luminous behind rooftops and steeples, visible from any point in the city.

The family strolled over to Riesengasse to see the presentation of giants from Tyrolean myths and legends, then on to Kiebachgasse to see the medieval houses and the fairy tale performances, from "Snow White and the Seven Dwarfs" to "Cinderella" to "Pinocchio." Later they saw a group of fire dancers called das Spielvolk, dressed as medieval courtiers spinning batons of real fire and fireworks.

At a Kiachl stand, Mama said, "Friedrich, shall we stop? Nicole hasn't had any Kiachl this season yet. Can you imagine that?"

"Well!" he huffed. "That's very disturbing. Nicole?"

"Yes, Papa, I would love some, with lingonberry jam and powdered sugar, please. We think you and Mama need to have some Glühwein with yours, too."

"Absolutely," Papa said. "Nothing like a hot cup of good cheer to sweeten the night."

"And the lingonberry jam has lots of vitamin C," Mama said. "Although I think the sauerkraut has more."

As the sun dipped below the mountain peaks, a full moon glowed in the firmament. The bells of Saint Jacob Cathedral rang five times, the last gong fading gently in the twilight. They walked over to the life-sized Nativity scene, where three-dimensional figures moved amid a waterfall and angels hovering behind clouds. At exactly five-thirty, the sound of trumpets burst into the evening air from the fifteenth century balcony under the Golden Roof. It was time for the daily Christmas concert.

"Papa, wouldn't it be nice if you played your trumpet here?" Nicole said.

He put his hand on her shoulder. "I have played here," he said. "But these days I have a few weekend and midweek concerts, and that's just enough for a busy family."

"Are we still going to your concert tomorrow afternoon?"

"If you'd like to. It should be very nice, we're playing at the Sandwirt Innsbruck. You've been there."

"Lots of times," Nicole said. She became aware of

Ashley tugging at her sleeve. She felt annoyed, but since Ashley wasn't saying anything, she figured she should wait to speak. She eased sideways to follow Ashley's tug.

"Nicole, let's move over here a little bit," she said softly. "We'll get a better view."

Nicole looked at Ashley quizzically, wondering what on earth she was up to now.

"It's okay," Mama said. "Just don't go too far. We're going to dinner soon."

Ashley pulled Nicole aside and huddled with her. "Look over there. See?"

Nicole looked through the crowd at a couple standing together and holding hands. "Is that Aunt Valeria?"

"Who else would wear such shoes? Oh my gosh! They're kissing. It's Mr. Bouchon. They're really kissing. Shall we tell Mama?"

"Are you going to start tattling now?"

"It's not tattling. It's just telling."

"Oh, hush yourself. Let's finish the concert so we can go have dinner. I'm already hungry again."

SUNDAY MORNING NICOLE was up with the sun. It was exactly two weeks before Christmas. She had slept with her door open so that she could smell the Christmas tree all night. When they came home from dinner last night, Papa and Mama had strung white lights on the tree to the sound of Christmas music. Together they had a collection of hundreds of carols from most countries in the world. The girls coached from all angles to make sure the lights were perfectly even. Right after the lights went the candy canes. Then Papa went into the Christmas closet and took out the tin of cookie cutters. Inside were also special recipes for cookies, some written in Grandma's handwriting, and others in Grandma Kinders' handwriting before she died. Papa had laminated them in clear plastic so they would be preserved. After Papa's Sunday concert would be cookie baking time. And while the cookies cooled, everybody would decorate the tree with the family's beloved collection of ornaments.

Also last night, Papa and Mama wrote Christmas cards and Nicole began writing her thank-you cards. She had received 33 gifts in the hospital from known people, and she organized her list into three groups of 11 cards to make the writing task easier. She checked with Ashley to make sure they would each send Mr. Bouchon a different card to thank him for the teddy bear and for the Advent calendar. She finished the first group last night, and today she would do another eleven. She enjoyed writing thank-you notes, because she thought about how happy the people would be to know how much she enjoyed their gifts. "Dear Innsbruck Police," she wrote. "I want to thank you kindly for the wonderful flowers you sent me when I was in the hospital. They were really beautiful and helped me to get well. Most of all I want to thank you for coming to save my life. I hope you all have a wonderful Christmas without too many emergencies. Yours, Nicole Kinders."

Each one she wrote, she carefully put into an envelope and wrote out the address from Papa's computer-printed address sheet. Finally she began her thank-you note to Mr. Brunheim. "Dear Mr. Brunheim, I wish to thank you and your sons kindly for the fast help you gave me when my house was on fire, and Mrs. Brunheim for calling emergency. You stopped everything you were doing to help. I was sick and you found me a blanket to keep warm. You don't know how much I appreciate you all for putting out the fire. But most of all I wish to thank you for Blitzen. I am heartbroken that he is gone. We tried to keep each other warm in the blizzard. I hope God blesses you always. Yours, Nicole Kinders."

Done for today, she thought as she addressed the last envelope. Time to wake Ashley up and get dressed for church. Monday she would do the last batch, which was the day Mr. Bouchon would be coming to put up the Advent calendar. She loved the music box carousel he had made last year, and she couldn't wait to see all twenty-five of his enchanted creations for the days of Advent.

It was going to be strange to go to school after being absent for a week, even though she was eager to get back into her normal routine after so much adventure. Aunt Valeria often said, "Too much adventure can dry out a girl's skin." There had been so much coverage of Nicole's adventure on TV and radio that her parents decided to avoid the news. For the days that Nicole was in the hospital, there were at least eight calls and visits to the house from TV personalities who wanted interviews with her, and that was while anybody was at home. Mama thought it would be inviting trouble for a young girl to be so well-known. "I'll be glad to keep you updated," Mama said, "but Nicole is still a child and isn't fond of being the center of attention." Papa agreed. "We only have to fight the news folks off for a week or so," he said. "After that they'll forget all about us."

❧ 14 ❧

After All

ON THE WAY home from church in Mama's car, Ashley was practicing her whistle. A new tooth was growing slowly into the gap in her smile, but much too slowly for her whistle to sound melodious.

Nicole was becoming annoyed. "Papa, could you turn on some music?" she said.

"I suppose we could."

"Papa — wait," Ashley said. "I first wanted to ask you if you knew any more stories to tell."

"Well, funny you should ask," he said. "Just this morning I was thinking of telling you about the poor mountain man, but it's a story Mama knows better than I do. Julia, would you like to tell them?"

"Please, Mama!" Nicole said.

"Well," Mama said, "let me think. Did I ever tell you?"

"No," they both said at once.

"Okay, then I will tell you. So there was this poor mountain man who lived all alone in the forest. He would hunt for his food, and he picked nuts and berries, and he would make tea from pine needles. Sometimes he would walk for a day to get into town. He was very poor, and had almost no money, just two or three silver coins under a stone in his hearth."

"What was his name?" Ashley asked.

"It was Holzmann," she said. "That's what everybody called him — Holzmann. He lived in a tiny house he built with his own hands from logs and stones. He had a fireplace that he used for heat and cooking. When fall came, he gathered all the nuts and roots he could, like chestnuts, carrots and potatoes. Anything that could last for a long time. But when winter came, he had to use only a little bit of food each day to make sure it would last.

"Sometimes it would snow so much that he couldn't even open his door. He had stacks of wood in his house to make sure he could keep a fire going. That was his biggest job in winter, to keep a warm home and have enough to eat. Now it was getting to be Christmas time, and a huge snowstorm came that covered all the land with snow for two days."

Nicole huddled her arms close to herself, her hands curled under her chin. "It's making me shiver," she said.

"Me too," Ashley said.

"Do you need me to stop?" asked Mama.

"No!" Nicole said. "Tell us more."

"Okay. So Holzmann was snowbound, and he was going to be stranded in his little hovel. He built his fire, not very warm but just enough to cook his little pot of soup. Just as he was ready to put his soup into a bowl to eat it, there came a knock on his door."

Papa knocked four times on the dashboard.

Mama paused for effect, then continued. "He couldn't imagine who could be at his door in the middle of the mountains, in the middle of winter, in all that snow. He got up and went to the door, and when he opened it he saw a young boy dressed all in furs. The boy was covered in snow. 'Could I please come in for some shelter?' he asked.

"Holzmann let the boy in, and asked 'What brings you here in this raging storm?' The boy said, 'I am a traveler, and I am going from town to town. I saw the smoke coming from your chimney and came here for shelter.' Holzmann asked him, 'Have you eaten?' And the boy said, 'I have not had food in two days.'

"So Holzmann said, 'All I have is this small pot of soup. If you gather me some snow outside, I can add it to the soup and we can divide it between us.' The boy opened the door just enough to reach outside, and he took a big handful of snow and put it into the pot. Soon the soup was boiling, and Holzmann took his cup and his bowl — he had very few kitchen things — and he divided the soup into each of them. He gave the bowl to the boy and said, 'Eat.' Well, somehow all the little pieces of vegetables and chestnuts that he put in it grew bigger while they were cooking. It was the most delicious soup, and both of them were satisfied.

"Then it came time to sleep. Holzmann was not used to company, so he slept in his corner of the hearth, and the boy slept in the other corner. In the morning, the boy opened the door and the sun was shining brightly. 'I must continue my journey,' he said. 'But before I go, I shall bless you and your home with abundance always. For I knocked, and you opened the door to me. I was hungry, and you gave me of your substance and not merely the scraps. And I was cold, and you gave me shelter. For this generosity your pocket shall never be without a coin, and your hearth shall always be warm, and your pot shall always have food.'"

Nicole looked at her mother's reflection in the rearview mirror and saw a smile she would remember always. "Wow, Mama. The Christ child came in disguise."

"That was the most excellent story," Ashley said. "I didn't even know we were already parked at home."

"Come now, everybody. Let's have some brunch so we can go to Papa's concert. And Nicole — there's something you might want to catch up on before we go."

"Did I forget something?" she asked.

"Well, yes. Remember all those gifts of kindness you passed on to other children at the hospital? And the good deeds you've done this Advent? Well, there's a manger that could use more straw for when the Christ child comes to our home."

"Oh! I was thinking about that yesterday. Thanks for reminding me," she said. "And I think Ashley might want to add some, too."

❀

ON THE LAST DAY of school before Christmas break, there was to be a concert by the student chorus and orchestra. The concert director, Mrs. Buchheit, appeared breathless at the door of Mr. Ziller's classroom and knocked. "Excuse me, Mr. Ziller. So sorry to interrupt you."

"That is fine, is there a problem?"

"We have eight chorus members out with the flu, and we need some students to fill in. Are there any people in the class who can sing in German, French and English?"

Three students raised their hands: two of them

were Nicole Kinders and Maximillian Brunheim. They looked at each other. Max raised his eyebrows, the new scar a fetching addition to his rosy face. Nicole could not help smiling, and raised her eyebrows, too.

"Would you like to stand in?" Mrs. Buchheit said. "We have music books for all the songs."

Nicole nodded. "Yes, I'll try. Will Isabelle Schubert be playing the piano?"

"Yes, of course."

"Well then, I'll definitely be there. I always wanted to sing whenever I heard Isabelle playing." She turned around and saw Isabelle beaming in her seat. "And Max, too. He has a very good voice, and we'll be glad to fill in."

"Please meet in the auditorium immediately after lunch period," Mrs. Buchheit said. "Thank you, Mr. Ziller."

Max turned to Nicole and whispered, "Good voice? I sound like a frog."

"Hush yourself. Practice makes perfect," she whispered back. "Make this a Christmas you'll remember."

For the first time in her life, Nicole felt what it was like to be on stage like Papa. Even though she wasn't trained in the songs, she knew them well enough to carry each one and follow Mrs. Buchheit's hand directions. Isabelle Schubert was positively shining on the school's baby grand piano, and the school orchestra was strong even though two members were absent.

Being part of the concert made Nicole want to join the school chorus. Somehow every song seemed bigger when she could sing it and hear it at the same time. She was close enough to hear Max singing among the boys, and though he didn't have such a good voice, he didn't hurt the concert either.

The last song was the old carol, "Fröhliche Weihnacht überall." Nicole knew it well from her youngest days, and she had heard the Vienna Boys Choir sing it at the concert. The student orchestra outdid themselves with the strings, wind instruments and bells, and the chorus held their harmonies and volume to the last ringing note. There was a pause after the end of the song when all the audience sat wide-eyed in the amazement of having just seen something beyond expectation.

Then in the middle of the auditorium a girl jumped to her feet and shouted, "Bravo!" Nicole could not see who it was, but the voice was unmistakably Ashley's. Immediately the entire school population was clapping enthusiastically. Mrs. Buchheit directed the chorus to take a bow, and pointed to the orchestra to play again as the chorus filed neatly off the stage. Nicole felt a tremendous pleasure coursing through her, and she realized what Papa's music teacher, Mr. Bernard, meant when he said, "I don't play the music because I'm happy. I am happy because I play the music."

❦

BY THE TIME Christmas Eve came, Nicole's golf ball bruise had healed almost completely. A follow-up doctor's appointment and X-ray showed no lasting problems from either the injury or the hypothermia. She was still in one piece, and ready for her school vacation that would last until January 6.

Papa came home with a magnificent gift basket almost too large for one person to carry. "This is a day to make a personal visit," he said.

"What in the world is that?" Mama asked.

"This basket has goodies from England, Ireland, France, Italy, Switzerland, Sweden, Portugal, Spain, Belgium, Norway, Denmark, Russia, Israel, Kuwait, India, Pakistan, China, Japan, Morocco, United States, Cuba, Puerto Rico, Brazil and Vietnam."

"Did you leave anybody out?" Mama said.

"Probably, but I was running out of air," he said.

"Oops," Mama said. "You left out Austria. We need to add some of our homemade cookies!" She got a gift tin of cookies and tucked it under the cellophane wrap of the basket.

"Now you girls know it's an old Austrian tradition for people to make house visits today," Papa said. "I owe a special visit to the Brunheims, to give thanks for everything they've done for us. Who wants to join me?"

Nicole and Ashley looked at each other and shrugged. "I'll go," Ashley said.

"I think I'll stay and help Mama set the table," Nicole said. She watched Papa and Ashley leave, and after the front door had closed, she realized that she, more than anybody, ought to be making a Christmas Eve visit. After all, Max had come on his own to visit her and apologize. And he did let her bamboozle him into singing in the school chorus. And she was curious about his eyebrow.

She hurried into her coat and boots, and ran out the front door too late to ride in Papa's car, as it had already gone out of sight. She sprinted as fast as her legs could carry her, getting to the big farmhouse just as Mr. Brunheim was opening the front door to let Papa and Ashley in with the huge basket.

"Wait for me!" she shouted breathlessly. It was strange to be around the Brunheim house without Blitzen jumping about and annoying her.

"Konrad, my friend," Papa said. "We would like to give you this present in thanks for all your family has done for us through the year, and especially this month."

"My, my, my! Thank you kindly, Friedrich. I'm sure we will enjoy this for a long time."

Mrs. Brunheim put a hand up to her red hair and smiled brightly. "Oh goodness, Merry Christmas to you, too! We just put up our Tannenbaum this morning. Would you like to come in and see?"

Nicole nodded. Everybody went into the parlor, and all the Brunheim boys were there. Karl was on his laptop computer, Stefan and Andreas were shaking gifts trying to guess their contents, and Max was putting candy canes on the tree. The boys all stood at attention when Papa entered the room with the girls. "Merry Christmas," they said.

"Merry Christmas to you all," Papa said. "We just want to thank you again for your help."

"These are goodies from all over the world," Ashley said, holding her hands out as if she were presenting a prize on a television contest show.

Nicole stood near the tree, noticing the candy canes hanging among the many antique ornaments. She was close enough to Max to notice a peach fuzz moustache beginning above his lip. He caught her looking at him and returned her gaze. His black eye was mostly healed, and his eyebrow had a permanent crease through it that looked like something a pirate would have. "I got you a little something," Max said.

"Really?"

"Well — I was going to bring it to you. Come, I'll show you."

She followed him out of the parlor into the front hallway. On the table that held the big clapper bell were a bunch of wrapped presents. Nicole felt awkward standing there while everybody else was talking in the parlor, but it gave her time to look at Max's dark hair curling about his forehead. He reached over to the table and picked out one of the wrapped packages. There was no ribbon or bow on it, just the word, "Nicole" hand-printed in shadowed box letters.

"Shall I open it now?" she asked.

"Sure."

She opened the package and inside was a SpongeBob banana toy, bright yellow plush with a goofy cartoon smile. "Oh my gosh," she laughed. "You didn't."

"For your karate practice," he said.

"You're a very bad boy, Max Brun —" she said, but was stopped by a sudden kiss directly on her cheek, right at the corner of her lips. She straightened up, a little surprised and a lot flabbergasted. She looked directly into his dark eyes and realized that she had just gotten her very first kiss from the very last boy on planet Earth she would expect it from. She put a finger to her cheek, then curled her hand up just below her throat.

"I hope you have the best Christmas ever," he said.

"I am having the best Christmas ever," she smiled. She was just ready to return his kiss when Papa and Ashley came out of the parlor. It would have to wait, but at least there was school vacation for two weeks.

"Okay, girls," Papa said. "Time to go home and help set up for our big feast!"

THERE WASN'T MUCH left to do by way of preparation when they arrived home from Christmas Eve Mass. The table had been set with the best china and crystal glassware, Christmas napkins, white candles and a centerpiece of Marcel Bouchon's Nativity piece, all perfectly placed. Papa's trumpet was in the parlor, ready for action. The tree stood fragrant and unlit, awaiting the magical moment after dinner when the manger full of hay would be brought in and placed in the stable. Nicole and Ashley were dressed in brand new holiday outfits and hairdos, and each had fingernails polished and ornamented.

Grandma and Grandpa were first to arrive. Ashley rushed to the door and was trying not to be overly excited, but the wreath still bounced when she pulled the door open. "Merry Christmas!" she chimed, and threw her arms around Grandma.

Nicole hurried to the entryway. As soon as Grandpa put down his two shopping bundles crammed with presents, she jumped up into his arms and gave him a bear hug. "Happy Christmas, Grandpa!"

"My goodness!" he said. "This is already the happiest Christmas in almost a hundred years, and it's only the beginning." He rubbed noses with Nicole, then let her back down on her feet.

"Now let me take a picture of you girls," Grandma said. "Just look how pretty! You are the loveliest young ladies in all of Austria."

"Thank you, Grandma."

The doorbell rang again, and in came Marcel Bouchon dressed in a red silk shirt and a designer holiday necktie, followed by Aunt Valeria, who breezed in sporting a lush green velvet dress and accompanying shoes, carrying a shopping bundle loaded with goodies.

Almost a half hour passed before Uncle Johan arrived. Tall and handsome, he looked as much like Grandma as he did like Grandpa. He wore a blue shirt with a bright red Jerry Garcia holiday necktie. He came in alone, and spoke for a while with Mama. It turned out that he and Pascale had to stop twice, because Pascale had developed carsickness since she became pregnant. Grandma and Mama hurried out to the car to help Pascale, and when she came in she looked pale but relieved to be off the road. Grandma made her some boiled water and served it in a delicate teacup. Uncle Johan was patting her shoulders from behind.

Even though Nicole knew the parlor was off limits till after dinner, she crept in and took a candy cane from the tree. She brought it to Pascale and whispered, "This might help."

"Thank you," Pascale said. She unwrapped the candy cane and tasted it. "Is this one of those magical candy canes that your uncle was telling me about?"

Nicole nodded. She liked Pascale's hair, bobbed with soft curls at her neck and a side part, with the top sweeping across her forehead. She reminded Nicole of those models from Paris and Rome in Mama's magazines.

Ashley came with a steaming hand towel that she was folding neatly into thirds. "Here, Aunty Pascale. You should put this over your forehead and rest for twenty minutes."

"That sounds wonderful," she smiled, her sapphire eyes brightening. "You're all making me feel so much at home. And just look at you girls! You've grown so much since I last saw you."

"Come now," Uncle Johan said. "Let's get your feet up and let you settle."

❦

THERE WAS NO shortage of feasting for everybody who could possibly fit around the table for Christmas Eve dinner. Everything from fried carp to gourmet potato dumplings, escargot for the adventurous, stuffed mushrooms, stuffed escarole, artichokes, farm cheese from the Brunheims, sweet yams with American maple syrup, and three kinds of olives from Greece, Italy and Spain served with crusty baguettes warmed in the oven. Afterwards Mama and Aunt Valeria brought out coffee and teas along with an original chocolate and apricot Sachertorte, complete with the customary whipped cream, followed by homemade Christmas cookies crafted mostly by Nicole and Ashley.

Pascale had rallied after her rest and gained back her appetite. Uncle Johan and Aunt Valeria told stories about adventures they'd had with Mama when they were children. Marcel Bouchon told a story about the first fish he caught when he was seven years old, and how the fish was so big it dragged him face-first into the water until his father pulled him out and helped him land the fish. "My Papa said I was the first under-water fisherman," he said.

After a story from Grandpa and Grandma, Pascale told her story about how she put her cell phone through the washing machine after she first met Uncle Johan, and couldn't get his call for what was supposed to be their first date. "Then a week later we bumped into each other in the post office," she said, reaching over to hold his hand. "I told him about my phone and we had a good laugh, and we went out that same night."

Then all the company moved into the parlor. Papa asked everybody to be very quiet as Mama carried the birch manger full of hay into the room and placed it in the stable beneath the tree. Papa turned on the switch and the tree instantly sparkled from the star on top to the lowest branches, reflecting against the outside darkness in the picture window, and filling the room with soft light.

It was a night of Nativity stories, carols, and exchanging presents for all. Nicole relished every moment, and knew deep in her heart that this Christmas was going to shine in her memory all the days of her life.

Special Recipes

Photo courtesy Masse's Pastries, Berkeley, CA.

Linzer Pig Cookies

You'll need a pig cookie cutter and a small heart cookie cutter, which are easy to find on the Internet.

1 cup unsalted hazelnuts or almonds or pecans
½ cup cornstarch
1½ cups (3 sticks) butter, softened (use only real butter!)
1⅓ cups confectioners' sugar
2 teaspoons vanilla extract or 1 teaspoon dry
  vanilla powder
¾ teaspoon salt
1 large egg
2¾ cups all-purpose flour
Seedless raspberry or apricot jam

1. In food processor with knife blade attached, pulse nuts and cornstarch until nuts are finely ground.

2. In large bowl, add butter and 1 cup of confectioners' sugar. Beat with mixer on low speed. Increase speed to high and beat 2 minutes or until light and fluffy, occasionally scraping bowl with a rubber spatula.

3. Set mixer to medium speed; beat in vanilla, salt, and egg. Reduce speed to low; gradually beat in flour and nut mixture just until blended, occasionally scraping bowl.

4. Take dough out of bowl and form a loaf on wax paper. Cut dough into 4 equal pieces, and flatten

each piece into a disk. Wrap each disk with plastic wrap and refrigerate 3 hours or until dough is firm enough to roll.

5. Preheat oven to 325 degrees F (165 degrees C). Take one disk of dough from refrigerator. On lightly floured surface, roll dough ¼ inch thick. Take the pig-shaped cookie cutter and cut as many pigs as you can from the sheet. Each finished cookie takes two pigs. Take the small heart-shaped cutter and cut a heart in half of the pigs. With floured

spatula, carefully place cookies, 1 inch apart, on ungreased large cookie sheet.

6. Bake cookies 17 minutes or until edges are lightly browned. Cool cookies on wire rack.

7. Dust the top cookies (with heart cutouts) with the remaining confectioners' sugar. A small tea strainer makes a good distributor if you fill it halfway and tap it gently over the cookies.

8. Spread a teaspoon of jam on bottom cookies using the back of the spoon for a paddle. Then place cutout cookies on top. You may need to match the cookies before adding jam, as some tails or feet may move or break during handling. Jam makes good glue, so don't worry.

9. Store the cookies in an airtight container with wax paper between layers. They will stay fresh for a week, longer if refrigerated. You may freeze the cookies, but they will need an extra dash of confectioners' sugar after thawing.

Easy Linzer Pig Cookies

For those who are just starting out with cookie baking, there's a simple way to make delicious Linzer-style cookies. You'll still need a pig cookie cutter and a small heart cookie cutter, which are easy to find on the Internet.

1 cup butter (2 sticks), softened
1 cup sugar
1 egg
1 teaspoon vanilla
1 tablespoon orange or lemon zest
2 teaspoons baking powder
3 cups all-purpose flour
⅓ cup confectioners' sugar for decoration
Seedless raspberry or apricot jam

1. In a large bowl, mix butter and sugar together. Add the egg, vanilla, and orange or lemon zest. Mix well until creamy. Sift the flour and baking powder together, then add slowly to the butter mixture. You will need to mix this by hand.

2. Preheat oven to 375 degrees F (190 degrees C). This dough does not need to be chilled before rolling. Roll out dough to ¼ inch on lightly floured surface.

3. Cut out as many pig shapes as you can from the sheet, and carefully place half of them on a

cookie sheet. Cut out a heart shape in each of the remaining half of the pigs, and remove the cutouts to add back to the dough leftovers for the next rolling. Now place these pigs on the cookie sheet.

4. Bake for 6–8 minutes or until lightly browned. Let the cookies cool slightly before placing them on a cooling rack.

5. Spread a teaspoon of jam on bottom cookies using the back of the spoon for a paddle. Then place cutout cookies on top. You may need to match the cookies before adding jam, as some tails or feet may move or break during handling. Jam makes good glue, so don't worry.

Chef Paul Masse preparing cookies.

6. Sprinkle confectioners' sugar over the finished cookies. A tea strainer makes a good distributor of confectioners' sugar if you fill it halfway and tap it gently over the cookies.

7. Try to save a few cookies to share, if possible.

Magic Hot Chocolate

Here's a recipe for perfect hot chocolate to warm you up on a wintry day.

Hot chocolate mix
Candy canes
Whipped heavy cream or Cool Whip
   (canned whip melts too fast)
Dash of cinnamon
Dash of nutmeg
Peppermint sprinkles if desired

1. Prepare the hot chocolate according to your favorite style, and leave room at the top for whipped cream. You can also use Marshmallow Fluff if you prefer, or mini marshmallows.
2. Add a dash of cinnamon and nutmeg, or peppermint sprinkles on top.
3. Unwrap a candy cane and use it for a stirrer. It will melt into the hot chocolate and add a nice peppermint flavor.

Photo courtesy Masse's Pastries, Berkeley, CA.

Saint Nicholas Cookies

These are wonderful spice cookies that are traditional in many countries. In Austria the cookie is called "Speculatius," which means "image."

You can get Saint Nicholas cookie cutters and special cookie decoration papers from the St. Nicholas Center Shop on the Internet at this address:

www.stnicholascenter.org/pages/cookie-papers

3 cups all purpose flour
1 ½ teaspoons baking powder
¾ teaspoon baking soda
¼ teaspoon salt
1 tablespoon ground ginger
1 ¾ teaspoons ground cinnamon
¼ teaspoon ground cloves
⅓ cup unsalted butter, softened
1 large egg
½ cup molasses
¾ cup packed brown sugar
2 teaspoons vanilla
1 teaspoon grated lemon zest

1. In a large bowl, whisk together flour, spices, baking powder and baking soda.
2. In an electric mixer bowl, beat together butter, brown sugar and egg with mixer on medium.

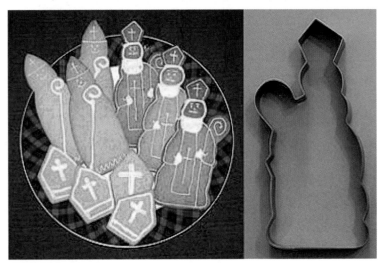

Photos courtesy of St. Nicholas Center   ❄   www.stnicholascenter.org

3. Add vanilla, molasses and lemon zest to the butter mix and blend well.
4. Add dry ingredients little by little and mix to form firm dough.
5. Refrigerate 2 hours.
6. Preheat oven to 350 degrees F (175 degrees C).
7. Roll dough to ¼ inch and cut out Saint Nicholas shapes. Place on paper-lined cookie sheets and bake for 12–13 minutes.

If you wish to use St. Nicholas papers to decorate the cookies, you can paste them on with a little apple jelly or thin glaze. The papers usually come with instructions and recipes. DO NOT eat the papers! Peel them off the cookies first. You may prefer to decorate the cookies by hand with white icing.

Icing for Saint Nicholas Cookies

¼ cup pasteurized egg whites (DO NOT use raw egg whites)
1⅓ cups confectioners' sugar
Cream of tartar

Beat sugar and cream of tartar into egg whites. You can adjust the consistency with more or less sugar.

You may use your own recipe for icing, or a prepared brand from your supermarket.

Kiachl

Sort of a cross between fried dough and a doughnut, Kiachl (KEYuh-kul) is a popular treat in the Christmas Markets of Austria. The easiest way to make Kiachl is to use prepackaged pizza dough, which saves time but has less flavor. Traditional Kiachl is made with brandy or rum and anisette in the dough, which adds a brighter flavor (don't worry, the alcohol disappears upon cooking).

2½ cups all-purpose flour
¼ cup sugar
3 packets yeast
¾ cup milk (lukewarm)
2 tablespoons melted butter (lukewarm)
2 eggs
1 teaspoon vanilla
2 tablespoons rum or brandy
1 tablespoon anisette or ¼ teaspoon anise flavoring
½ teaspoon grated lemon zest (optional)
Pinch of salt
Vegetable oil for deep-frying

1. Mix all the ingredients in a large bowl, stirring thoroughly with a wooden spoon. The dough will be soft. Cover the bowl and put in a warm place for about an hour till the dough doubles in size.

2. If you are using pizza dough, let it rise till the dough doubles in size.

3. Now separate the dough into egg-sized pieces, and place them on a floured cookie sheet or pastry board. It may be sticky, so be patient. Let set for 10 minutes.

4. Heat cooking oil on medium and test with a toothpick. If bubbles rise, the oil is hot enough.

5. Form a Kiachl by taking one floured piece and pressing an indentation in the center while forming a thicker outside edge, as if you had formed it over a kneecap.

6. Place the dough carefully into the hot oil and let it fry till golden brown on one side. Then turn it over in the oil and let it finish on the other side.

7. Remove from oil and place on paper toweling to absorb excess oil.

Kiachl Fillings

Lingonberry jam*
Sauerkraut
Nutella spread
Confectioners' sugar

You may add lingonberry jam ("Preiselbeeren" in German) or Nutella spread in the center indentation. Kiachl is also delicious plain. Sprinkle with confectioners' sugar and serve warm.

If you prefer sauerkraut, no need to add confectioners' sugar. Kiachl with sauerkraut is also good with sausage, meat, or fish dishes.

*Lingonberry jam is available at Ikea stores and on the Internet.

Photo courtesy Masse's Pastries, Berkeley, CA.

Chocolate Wreaths

This is a favorite for those who can't get enough chocolate in the winter. You'll need a Linzer cookie cutter set or a 3-inch fluted round cookie cutter and a 1-inch round cookie cutter.

> *1 cup (2 sticks) unsalted butter, softened*
> *½ cup sugar*
> *2 ounce packet bittersweet chocolate, melted*
> *2 cups all-purpose flour*

1. In electric mixer with paddle, beat sugar and butter together. Add melted bittersweet chocolate and beat until smooth.

2. Slowly mix in flour until dough forms.

3. Separate the dough into 2 disks, wrap in plastic and chill for about 1 hour.

4. Preheat oven to 325 degrees F (165 degrees C).

5. Roll dough on lightly floured surface to ¼ inch and cut out wreaths with the 3-inch fluted Linzer cookie cutter. If you have a 2-part Linzer cutter, put the small circle cutter in the center. If not, then use a 1-inch cutter to remove the centers. Place wreaths on an ungreased cookie sheet.

6. Bake for 20 minutes. Cool wreaths on a cooling rack.

Wreath Decoration

½ cup semi-sweet chocolate chips or Dolce chocolate, melted
Chocolate or colored sprinkles

Dip wreaths into melted chocolate and place on wax paper. Add chocolate or colored sprinkles and let cool.

A Note from the Author

The Taste of Snow began at a Christmas party held at the home of my dear friends, Lew and Irina Franklin. Toward the end of the party, their daughter Nicole asked me to tell her a story, and I came up with something about a girl and a magic candy cane. A few days later I received a Christmas card from Nicole which read, "A magic candy cane for you, too. Make that story a book. Your books rock!"

So I wish to thank Nicole Franklin for inspiring a story I never planned to write, and her sister Ashley for lending her face to Ashley Kinders.

I would also like to thank Samantha and Lauren Gill, cherished cousins who have provided me with a wealth of inspiration, entertainment, suggestions, and laughter since they were very small. Many thanks to their parents, Paul Gill and Anne Christopher, MD, who provided me with medical information as well as an audience of four wonderful children.

Thanks to Emma and Emilia Viggh, who introduced me to Barbapapa cartoons and showed me how to have a proper shut-up contest. And I mustn't forget Isabella Cammarata, who really can play the piano with her eyes closed.

Without technical support this book would probably not have made it to press. Carole Montone has used her insights and knowledge as a mother and editor to guide my writing with tact and support. Ron Chait is my copy editor, and I dare say he's one of the best. Also thanks to Paul Vasta for restoring my PC and finding a segment of the book that disappeared before backup.

A very special thanks to Brian Allen, who patiently worked with me through all the phases of illustration, both for the cover and the chapter headings.

And what kind of book would present Christmas baking without recipes? Paul and Marcia Masse of Masse's Pastries in Berkeley, California graciously provided recipes of some select holiday treats, with photos by Dee Conway. Jennifer Coulombe assisted with artistic design. Also thanks to the St. Nicholas Center for providing a delightful website with information, recipes and photos, and granting permission to use them in this book.

Thanks to Sharon Chait for the music, Henry F. Scannell for his part in keeping the Boston Public Library the remarkable place it is, Jerry Fireman, Greg Smutny, Susan Williams, Wayne Strattman, and many of the folks from Art2Art, who provided various venues for me to introduce my stories.

Family encouragement was always plentiful and much appreciated. A special tip of the hat to Mom & Dad, Mary & Jay, Bob & Alex, and John & Kathy. Also a salute to all my friends and acquaintances who provided support, ribs and brew at Redbones, and house parties to keep my social life alive through the snowiest winter in recent memory. You know who you are, and I thank you from the bottom of my heart.

Stephen V. Masse